FIRE WIZARD

Ghostspeaker Chronicles Book 4

PATTY JANSEN

GET FREE EBOOKS

Visit pattyjansen.com
to sign up for Patty's mailing list. You get four series
starter ebooks for free!

CHAPTER 1

A MAN'S VOICE shouted at the bow of the ship. The sound echoed over the water in the still afternoon air.

Johanna sat up, dazed. She'd been lazing on the sloping covers of the ship's hold, warmed by whatever little winter sunshine made its way over the hill on the western side of the river, and she must have fallen asleep.

She'd been exhausted.

With her overnight trip to the farm of the Guentherite order, she had barely slept the previous night, and after their frantic escape from Florisheim, both the *Lady Sara* and the *Prosperity* had settled into a steady drift down the swollen river. There had been little for the refugees to do except rest.

Until now, that was.

Ko, at the bow, had pulled in the team of sea cows and was directing them to the riverbank. Johanna let herself slide down the sloping cover and went up the front to join him.

They were in a bend in the river, and forest on the high

bank had been cleared to make room for . . . yes, what exactly?

Or rather, what had it been?

Because clearly some disaster had happened recently, maybe as recently as last night, judging by the churned earth and the splintered stumps of wood that were still smouldering.

The jumble of broken and shattered buildings stretched over most of the lower part of the sloping riverbank on the left hand side. A stately house surrounded by vineyards at the top of the hill remained untouched, but every other structure closer to the river was reduced to a pile of smoking rubble.

A blue haze hung low over the ground.

In between the wreckage lay mounds of dirt. There were a couple of carts, torn to shreds, and the body of a horse. Overnight wild animals had ripped part of its belly open, spilling blood and entrails on the blackened ground.

"What is this place?" Johanna asked.

"This is the Guentherite abbot's summer residence," Ko said, his face white. He stared at the scene, his mouth open.

"The place where you were captured?"

"The very place. When you sent us to check on Saardam, we came down the river and saw all this activity here. There were people with boats, and there was a jetty over there."

All that remained were shattered pylons.

"We didn't know what to do so we pulled the boat to the bank, but it was a poor hiding place."

Both riverbanks were too steep for reed beds and there wouldn't have been anywhere for the men to hide.

"I'm guessing it didn't used to look like this."

"There used to be a couple of open sheds with carts." He pointed. "That over there was the caretaker's house, and over there was a large furnace."

Johanna remembered the furnace on the Guentherite brotherhood's farm. "For what?"

"Making iron."

"What do they want all this iron for?"

He shrugged. "They were making it into big blocks and sheets that they stored in a shed over there." But that shed no longer stood upright and Johanna could make out no iron in the rubble.

"Did many people live here?"

He nodded. "At least a hundred. Maybe more. I don't know. We never spent that much time here."

Johanna saw no one, not even dead people.

The two boats drifted towards the remains of the jetty. A couple of boys came with sticks and ropes to hold the boat off and tie it to the jetty.

"Hello!" someone yelled at the deck of the *Prosperity*. "Hello! Is anyone there? Hello! Do you need help?"

Something moved behind the dead horse. A man rose, leaning on a shovel. He probably climbed out of the grave that he had been digging. He stared wide-eyed at the two ships coming towards the shore. His hair was grey and dirty, his hands were black and he had smeared a black smudge over his face.

"Is he a monk?" Johanna asked. The man wore a drab grey garment that didn't look like a habit.

"Prisoner," Ko said, his voice dark.

"By himself? Why doesn't he run away?"

Ko met her eyes. "Because there is nowhere to run to? The forests around here are not kind. There are bears and wolves. Looking at the horse, the wolves have already been here. There are ghosts, too."

Maybe, but Johanna thought that the worst thing one had to fear in the forest was other people. Sylvan and his bandits roamed these places. She still didn't know for certain who had killed all those people and put them in the ice cellar.

The stories of the two scouts Ko and Willem had been told and retold many times: they had been captured when they went downriver to check on Saardam. They'd been taken to the Guentherite brotherhood's farm where they had been forced to dig black rock out of a deep hole in the mountainside. The hole was close to the river and constantly at risk of flooding, because water seeped through the rock. The monks used the water wheel to scoop it out, but still, the diggers stood in water all day. There had been many different people, mostly young men, mostly from downriver. Some were hapless farmers who had stumbled across one of the brotherhood's projects while going to market or moving their animals. Some were peddlers or merchants travelling on horseback from town to town. They'd found their horses and stock confiscated, their travel clothes removed and replaced with a grey sack-like garment. Others were people whose families owed the brotherhood debts from as far away as Burovia. They all worked in the hole together, and learned to communicate across languages.

It was always dangerous. When the water seeped through the black rock, it absorbed ghosts that had been disturbed by the digging activities. The ghosts would float between the workers, sometimes making them fall asleep on the spot, sometimes making them fight each other.

Once the black rock had been brought to the surface,

some of it would be used to light the furnace at the back of the chapel. In the furnace the monks would melt ore that came from upriver by boat, and turn it into iron. Both the bars of iron and the rest of the black rock would be shipped to the Abbot's summer residence along the river, and no one knew what happened to those materials there.

The lonely surviving man walked to the shore with a painful-looking gait and a distinct limp. He called something in a local dialect, waving his hands.

Johanna asked, "Does he want help or does he want us to go away?"

No one could answer that.

Karl, aboard the *Prosperity,* yelled something back at him and the man replied.

"He says we should move on as soon as possible," Karl yelled across the water to Johanna. "He says this is a dangerous place."

"Is there anyone else here?" she yelled back.

He asked the man and the man gave a longer reply, waving his hands and pointing. Karl looked up into the sky, frowning. He asked more questions and the man answered.

Roald said next to her, "He says that a great fire serpent came and burnt the place down."

Yes, that was true, he had spent time at the order. He would be able to understand their dialect.

"He says that the other people all ran into the forest and didn't come back. He says that he can't run because of his leg, so they left him behind."

"Did he say what sort of place this is, what they're making here?"

"No, but he keeps saying that we should leave because the fire serpent will be back."

The man kept looking at the sky.

"What is this fire serpent?"

"The fire serpent was mentioned in the books we read." Roald sounded indignant. "I showed you the pictures."

"But they are mythological creatures."

He gave her a *yes, and?* look.

Johanna remembered the dragons described in the book called *On The Magickal Creatures of the High Lands, the Sea and the Orient* that Roald had borrowed from the Jeromist monastery in Florisheim. There was no time to argue about what was real and what were folk tales. He was unlikely to understand the difference.

Then again, he had also told her that there was a dragon at the Guentherite farm, and that it used to sit on a brother's shoulder warning of bad air. She hadn't seen it when she went there, not that she'd looked for it. People seemed confused about what type of creature was called a dragon.

The conversation between Karl and the old man went on for a bit, and ended when the old man retreated up the riverbank. Short of rowing the dinghy to shore, the passengers couldn't have a closer look, and no one on board showed any inclination of wanting to do that. The women stood holding scarves over their noses. The air smelled of charred meat. They might not see any dead, but evidently the fire dragon had burned a lot of people.

Johanna beckoned for the old man to join the boats, but he seemed scared and not interested in coming on the boats, so they could do nothing except push off again.

The boats slowly drifted downstream while the man stood on the riverbank, watching and leaning on his shovel.

When there was a bend in the river and he vanished

from view, Johanna went downstairs and leafed through the book of magical creatures, but it gave her no more information than she already remembered. The book contained a drawing of a dragon, a scaled, snake-like creature with wings that were far too small for it to get off the ground.

While it was said that dragons breathed fire, this particular one looked like a lizard to her with some wings drawn on. She had seen lizards in Lurezia where people kept them as pets. A peddler at the markets had baskets full of them. Some were thin and lithe, others short and fat. He had picked one up and given it to her to hold. She remembered the heavy and smooth feel of the creature as it warmed itself on the palms of her hands. Lizards were harmless, and she was sure that the "dragon" Roald had referred to that was supposed to be at the Guentherite farm was really a lizard. A fire serpent, whatever that was, didn't sound harmless.

Johanna couldn't help thinking that the Guentherite order's digging activities in the ground had upset a lot of bad things.

Necromancy, ghosts released from the ground in such numbers that the water became murky, fire creatures. Evil wizards taking over peaceful lands.

And the boats were drifting on this sick and ghost-infested water, closer and closer to Saardam, where people had no magic, where a Guentherite wizard had taken up residence, and the only useful magic they had was Johanna's ability to see things in wood. The fact that wood burned in fire seemed a cruel coincidence.

CHAPTER 2

WINTER WAS COMING. It was in the crispness of the air, in the whiteness of the dew on the grass, almost but not quite frozen as rime. It was in the steam rising from the river and blowing out of the nostrils of the cows that stood on the riverbank and that raised their heads curiously as the two river boats drifted downstream.

Johanna could feel the winter in her bones. Still, she counted herself lucky that she had a bed to sleep in, and that she didn't have to lie on the floor, or even sit on the deck, covered only by a horse blanket. But even down in the ship's hold in the little cosy room she shared with Roald, it was damp and cold. She'd given the warm blanket to a mother with two young girls—they were asleep in the corner of the room under the stairs, the mother leaning against the wall and the girls with their heads in her lap.

Their cheeks were red, and Johanna hoped that the girls were warmer than she felt. She had mistakenly thought that Roald would keep her warm, but all he did at night was toss and snore and keep her awake, and now she was stiff and cold as well as tired.

When she came up on the deck, the temperature dropped even further. Shivering, she pulled the cloak closer around her. Her breath steamed in the air.

Loesie sat at the bow on the driver's bench, her legs pulled up under her. The rope that held the harnesses of the sea cows hung slack, because the ship had moored at a rickety jetty and the animals were grazing nearer the shore.

"How far do we still have to go?" Her voice sounded loud in that silence.

Loesie let out a gasp. Had she been asleep? She let her feet down from inside the blanket and stuffed them in her old boots.

"There," she said and pointed over the riverbank, between a couple of willow trees.

Squinting through the mist, Johanna tried to make out what Loesie was looking at. A concentration of trees. A few windmills. And on the horizon, the faint outline of a tower.

Saardam. "Is that it?"

"It is. I don't think we should go any further with the boats."

They had discussed this when mooring here last night, that they were not going to take the ships all the way into Saardam because no one knew what they'd find there.

The Nieland vessel lay in the next bay upriver, tied to a couple of trees. The *Prosperity* was both larger and had a larger deck, and it carried most of the refugees. Normally used for storing transport crates, they had planned to use the deck as seating area for Roald and Johanna's official wedding. How trivial that planning now seemed, and why had they been so addled by magic to even consider having the ceremony in Florisheim?

Magic.

She shuddered.

Everything in Florisheim had been steeped with magic. It had affected everyone's decisions.

Some people on the *Prosperity* were early risers, courtesy of the cooks and the former soldiers who had made it on board. Captain Arense, too, already stood on the deck. He was wearing his grey cape. Some children had taken the dinghy ashore and were coming back with a bucket of milk. They chattered with shrill and far too cheerful voices that made Johanna's head hurt. Maybe they'd slept better on board that ship. Maybe they were used to discomfort. Maybe it was because they were children and didn't feel the cold. Everyone had been exhausted. No doubt the coming days would be even more exhausting.

Johanna went down the *Lady Sara*'s gangplank and picked her way across the rotting planks of the jetty. It would be a place where farmers loaded their milk and cheese to take to the markets in Saardam. But judging by the weeds that grew in the cracks of the wood and the grass that pushed through the gaps from underneath, it had been a long time since anyone had used the jetty.

Johanna waded through the grass of the riverbank. It was cold and damp closer to the ground, and remnants of mist trailed over the grass. A couple of willow trees guarded the bank like silent sentinels. In passing, Johanna ran her hand over the weathered trunks, and saw peaceful grazing cows in a brilliant green paddock. At least nothing bad had happened here in recent months.

The rope holding the ship in place had been tied around one of the tree trunks, and the wood did show her a man going out in the dinghy to tie it. He pulled the dinghy up onto a little beach a few steps across, climbed up the bank, dragging the rope through the reeds, and looped it around the trunk.

When Johanna came to the little beach, Captain Arense himself came down the ladder. He pulled the dinghy close and rowed a few strokes to the shore.

"It is getting cold these days, Your Majesty," he said while helping her in.

"It certainly is." She longed to be in a warm room with a roaring fire. Her heart ached when she thought of her father, and that she would soon know whether he was still alive. In a way she feared to find out, because if the news was bad, she would be better off not knowing.

The oars splashed in the calm water.

The dinghy glided across and a moment later clonked into the side of the *Prosperity*'s hull. Captain Arense grabbed the rope ladder and held it down. Johanna clambered up, her hands stiff from the cold.

On the deck, a number of women stood huddled around a camp stove on which stood a huge pot. The little boys that Johanna had seen carrying the milk sat on the railing, eying the spoon going around and around in the porridge.

It smelled really good.

The door of the cabin opened and Johan Delacoeur stepped onto the deck. He was a tall man and he had to bend to avoid hitting his head against the top of the door-frame. He, too, looked a little the worse for wear, with a giant mud stain on his shirt that he must have acquired in the scramble to get on board.

He nodded when he saw Johanna, but his expression remained guarded. Did he remember how wrong he'd been about the Red Baron and the Baron's son's evil magic? Both his noble mates, Fleuris LaFontaine and Ignatius Hemeldinck had not made it onto either the *Prosperity* or the *Lady Sara*. There was no way of knowing whether they had survived, but Johanna guessed that they were probably with the Baron or staying with their cronies in Florisheim. Maybe they had seen the Baron's evil ways, but she didn't hold out too much hope. She didn't even think that Johan Delacoeur saw the truth. He was just here because of his family and because he happened to be in the camp when the panic broke out and his mates happened to be . . . elsewhere.

Johanna sat on the railing, waiting for the porridge to cook. Johan Delacoeur put his hands in his pockets and remained outside the door to the captain's cabin, looking ruffled and tired.

He yawned. "Pray, why have we stopped in this field?"

"Saardam is just over there." Johanna glanced at the western horizon, where pale sunlight touched the mist-covered meadows.

"Isn't that a reason to keep going?"

Johanna resisted the temptation to roll her eyes.

A woman handed Johanna porridge in a chipped bowl. "Be careful. It's very hot."

Johanna ate as quickly as she could, letting the hot goo make its way to her stomach.

The Shepherd Carolus had also come onto the deck, looking rumpled, unshaven and rubbing his face.

"So, when are we going to continue?" Johan Delacoeur asked the Shepherd. He held his bowl, untouched, as if eating porridge was beneath him.

"I thought you'd heard at the meeting last night that we're leaving the ships here." The Shepherd had been attending a sick child and had not heard all of the discussion last night.

"Ridiculous." Johan muttered under his breath.

The Shepherd gave him a startled and too-innocent look. "Why ridiculous? When the scouts return, they'll tell us how safe it is to go in. We'll be splitting up and going into town dressed as farmers and peddlers so that we don't attract attention."

Johan scoffed. "I'm not going to dress up in rags—"

"Oh, yes, dear, you are." This was his wife, Martine.

One of the younger girls said, "You can always be a pauper for real, like the rest of us."

Johan went red in the face. "I'm going to stay with the ship."

Martine said, "The boys are already doing that. They're much handier with sea cows than you are. We'll do whatever is necessary to go home. Aren't you keen to find out what has become of your sisters?"

He snorted, took a spoon full of porridge, burned his mouth, but ate it anyway, glaring at his wife.

Johanna was beginning to like Martine Delacoeur, who might be of noble birth, but didn't put up with any nonsense. She nodded at Johanna as if she wanted to say *Never mind him, we'll do whatever we want.*

It was a pity they didn't have children.

CHAPTER 3

ONE BY ONE, the fellow travellers came onto the deck, either from the *Prosperity*'s hold or ferried in the dinghy from the *Lady Sara*. There were eighty-two people on both vessels, men and women of all ages, but they were mostly from the middle and upper classes and their households.

The women at the stove doled out porridge, while their daughters climbed the rope ladder down to the water to rinse bowls and spoons because, between the inventories of the two ship kitchens, they didn't have enough of either.

Johanna remained out of the way and only moved to the ladder when Roald had decided to come up. His straw-blond hair was too long and messy and his beard had gotten quite long as well. He looked perfect for disguising himself as peasant.

She thought he looked cute and with pain in her heart remembered how happy he was when gardening or catching frogs, and how much he was unsuited to meetings, speeches and politics. One of the women gave him a bowl, and he ate, quietly and neatly, with a spoon, without slurping and without spilling, while standing next to Johanna, leaning against the railing.

On the deck, the word went around that Saardam was visible from the *Lady Sara*'s position and young Gijsbert and his little friends hoisted each other on top of the cabin to have a look. They reported that it was really misty. Some blue sky peeped through the mist directly overhead, heralding a sunny day. A flock of geese flew high up there, on their way south for winter. Roald was looking at them, too.

"Winter is coming," he said.

Johanna nodded and touched his hand. He looked tense, unused to sharing his home with so many people. His need to be alone and on the riverbank, looking for birds and frogs, radiated off him.

The young boy Gijsbert called out, "Look, they're back!"

He stood on the roof of the cabin, pointing at the riverbank, where the two scouts that had gone out that morning were wading through the grass back towards the boats.

The captain sent out the dinghy and the two, Dirk and Jan, brothers and the sons of a merchant, were hauled up the ladder. Everyone crowded around them, wanting to know how things were in Saardam and whether their houses were still standing.

"Give them some space and let them eat first," Master Deim said, waving people aside.

The two young men bowed to Johanna and Roald. "Your Majesties, we're back to report what we've seen in Saardam."

"Be at ease, and have some porridge first, while it's warm."

One of the women brought two bowls, which the men cradled in their hands. "It was cold out this morning," Dirk said.

This was followed by a tense silence while he and his brother ate. More and more people gathered on the deck, everyone keen to hear how their families or houses were.

Then Jan, the oldest and tallest of the two began, "When we got to the city gates at first light, there were two guards stationed at the gates, but they allowed us to pass without a glance. We weren't the only ones queued up to get into the city. People, like farmers and monks were all going in and out, most of them carrying things to sell." He went on to say that a lot of houses had been touched by the fire, but there were also many that had not. The destruction was in the middle of town, around the palace, the harbour and the markets. "But even there, some houses have strangely survived. It was almost as if some of the houses were made from stone and couldn't burn. You'd see two houses next to each other, and one would be burnt to cinders while the other was untouched."

"Witchcraft," someone muttered, and people nodded.

A lot of people then wanted to know about their houses in particular and did the brothers see anyone they knew? Master Deim had to call for people to calm down again.

"The only thing we can say for sure is that Joris DeCamp will have to find a new house. There is a queue of people waiting outside the door. It looks like the occupier and his cronies have taken up residence there."

"Is there any sign that they know that we're coming or

that the heir to the throne is still alive?" Master Deim asked.

The men shook their heads.

"The guards at the gate are pretty easy," Dirk said. "We spoke to some people on the streets. No one knows anything. And if Alexandre knew that we were coming, he would have put more men at the gates."

True.

"What about the palace?" someone asked, and Johanna wanted to know about this as well.

"Couldn't see anyone there. The gates are shut. The building looks damaged, but no one was there and no one has fixed it yet. The church is completely gone. That area is a wasteland of mud and rubble."

There were gasps at this.

A woman said, "But when we left, though it was badly damaged some of the walls were still standing. They could have put on a new roof."

"None of the occupiers would have been interested in restoring the church," Martine Delacoeur said. Johanna wasn't sure if she had ever gone to church, since most of the nobles were members of the Belaman Church, even if people in Saardam considered those two one and the same.

The Shepherd Carolus was shaking his head, a pained look on his face. He had his parish at a different church, and already knew that his church had been destroyed, too. "It is a monstrous thing. We have never harmed anyone, never encouraged a war, or tried to drive out others. We have always helped people—" He spread his hands.

The Church of the Triune helped *common* people and forbade magic, both things that would disturb the noble classes that ruled much of the low lands.

Dirk said, "It looks like they're building something

new where the church used to stand. There's blocks of stone and they're putting down trenches for the foundations."

People talked about what they thought was being built —a new palace, another church—

Johanna asked the scouts if they'd seen evidence of bandits or soldiers.

Jan said, "There are some, but unless a lot of Alexandre's men have left, the occupying army doesn't look very big. They use Saarlanders. We did see some bandits, one with a bear, but it's not like the streets are full of them."

That's because Alexandre uses magic.

At any rate, Johanna judged it safe to proceed with their plan.

She asked the women to pull out all the clothing they had. As coincidence had it, the *Prosperity* had been carrying a shipment of luxury goods when it fled Saardam. Some of its cargo included fabrics. In the previous months, women had used all of the fabrics to make clothes, and those items now looked a little the worse for wear, and perfect for the purpose of disguising as travellers or peddlers.

A few men went ashore and brought back two wheelbarrows with cabbages, eggs and some beetle-ridden dried beans from a nearby barn. One of them said, "It's a sad thing to have to do this, Your Majesty, but I guess the dead have no more use for food and wheelbarrows."

Johanna nodded, sadly, remembering the carnage they had seen at a few places along the river.

They had also collected apples, most of those worminfested. Johanna told the children to pick out the best ones, and that they could have the rest. Gijsbert, some older boys and a couple of girls bickered over who would get which apple and then went to great efforts to eat around the worms.

The first group of "farmers" left soon after, taken ashore by Captain Arense. There were five in the group, a father and a son and daughter, and the two brothers who had gone before. One of the young men took one wheelbarrow and bowed to Johanna and Roald on the deck of the *Prosperity*.

Johanna watched them disappear over the path on top of the levee with a feeling of apprehension. The thought that they were doing this for her made her feel sick. She'd been hungry this morning but now she felt so nervous that the porridge she had eaten might make its reappearance any time soon.

What if Alexandre's men knew they were coming and were waiting for them at the city gates? What if none of the people loyal to the royal family were still alive? After all, King Nicholaos hadn't made himself popular with influential people, and the nobles left in Saardam had decided they were better off without the royal family. What if there was nothing left to save? Were all these people risking their lives for nothing?

Not too much later, a group of six left, including Master Deim, Julianna Nieland and Shepherd Carolus. They were dressed in rags, some with burn holes, and their story would be that they came to look for work in Saardam after the destruction of their village.

And so they spread out and left in dribs and drabs, with some people planning to enter the city from the western gate in order to prevent the guards at the gate from getting suspicious.

Everyone would try to find their own family and their own houses. Those who found that impossible would meet at the end of the day at the Brouwer Company's sea cow barn, or, if the barn was no longer there, Master Deim's barn, which was on the next quay.

As the day progressed, the ships emptied of people. Johanna felt drained and slept a bit. Roald wanted to go into the reeds to catch frogs, and was upset that she told him that he could not, so he threw a fishing line over the side of the boat and leaned against the railing, moping. He caught two little fish.

By midday, none of the people had come back yet, so Johanna got changed into the peasant's dress that she had taken from the mill and that had sustained rips during the trek with the bandits. Nellie had since fixed it as best as she could.

Then she helped Roald get changed, too. He fidgeted and wouldn't keep still. She probably got a bit more impatient with him than was warranted. It was impossible to hurry Roald along. He did things at his pace or not at all.

"I don't like this shirt." He pulled at the collar which, to be honest, was a bit tight.

"You have to wear it anyway."

"I don't understand. Why are we leaving?"

"We're going back to the palace." If there was anything left of the palace.

"I don't want to go. I like the boat."

She sighed. In a way, she liked it, too. She liked it that it calmed him to be outside, pottering about near the water, catching frogs. She let her hands fall and looked around the cabin that had been their home for two months. The bed, the cosy desk with the Baron's books still on it. Oops.

There was also the jar that Roald used for holding

frogs. She remembered using it to scoop up the frog that had escaped.

"Why are you laughing?"

"I remembered trying to catch that frog."

"Oh, yes, the frog that got out."

It was sad. It was the end of their uncomplicated life.

CHAPTER 4

WHEN JOHANNA and Roald were ready to go, they climbed back onto the deck.

Roald looked quite like an unshaved peasant from a distance. Close up, people would see that his hands were clean and fine, and that his trousers were of a material that was too expensive for a peasant. Even Nellie in her old torn and stained dress no longer looked like a simple maid. And Loesie wore her dark farm dress, but the expression in her grey eyes was chilling. Johan Delacoeur refused to take off his jacket. It was plenty dirty, he said, as if being "dirty" was indicative of peasants. Martine wore one of the dresses that had been made out of the material that had been on board the *Prosperity*. Too fine, really, to make a convincing peasant dress. Johanna hoped that the guards wouldn't notice any of those things.

The six of them were meant to be farmers going to market, and they were to take the last wheelbarrow and cabbages and apples.

They descended to the dinghy and Captain Arense rowed them across.

"Good luck," he said in a grave voice when they were at the beach.

Johanna nodded.

Johan Delacoeur clapped him on the shoulder.

The captain would stay with his ship.

It was worrying to leave the *Lady Sara* behind. Yes, Ko and Willem would stay with the captain, but they were no real defence if someone wanted to take possession of the ships, and if they had no time to rig up the sea cows their only measure of escape—to simply cast off—would only take them into Saardam, where their problems might be worse than the ones they'd be trying to escape.

They distributed the farm produce. Johanna got a basket of eggs.

Roald was pretty good at wheelbarrows and pushing it gave him something to do. That was another thing about Roald: when he had something to do, he wouldn't panic and start swaying or squealing.

In this manner, they picked their way up the grassy side of the levee. The *Lady Sara* disappeared from sight. The day had turned sunny, if windy and crisp, and the breeze brought a muddy scent from the nearby lowlands. The trees had lost all their leaves and the wind whistled through the bare branches. The grass had started to yellow.

The group followed the track along the river, occasionally having to divert to avoid muddy areas. Clearly, the water had been high here, too.

They'd been walking for a while when Nellie said, "Wait, is that a horse?"

Johanna looked at the stand of willows where Nellie pointed. Strands of hair blew across her face.

A horse it was, with a brown coat. When Roald whistled, it came clopping through the paddock towards the group.

It was a fine animal, not suitable for the field. Its coat was unkempt, full of thistles and other seeds; it had likely fled the city during the fire. A coach horse, maybe. It had the reins still over its head, and that would have made it very uncomfortable. Not to mention that it was a wonder it hadn't become tangled somewhere. No bit fortunately, or it would have starved to death.

Roald put down the wheelbarrow and coaxed it close enough that he could grab the dangling reins. He lifted the headpiece off. The apple in his hand disappeared with a big crunch.

"What are we supposed to do with a horse?" Nellie asked.

Johanna said, "Take it into town. It belongs to someone there. Maybe we can sell it."

Roald said indignantly, "I found it. It's mine." He tied a piece of rope around the horse's neck.

Johanna guessed it could sleep in the barn, if the barn was still there, but it was one more thing to worry about.

The horse kept shying when Loesie came too close, so Johanna ended up taking the rope and leading it along.

The light was turning golden when the group finally arrived at the gates, which Johanna saw, to both her disappointment and relief, looked no different from when she had left. Wait—there was a difference: one of the towers on the gate flew an unfamiliar flag in blue and white.

Johan Delacoeur was looking at it, too, a frown on his face.

"Do you know the flag?"

He shook his head.

A small number of people were going in and out of the

gates, mostly farmers and other folk from out of town. The horse was getting nervous, so Roald put the headpiece back on and Loesie took the wheelbarrow from him while he led it.

They went up onto the bridge over the water.

The horse's hooves went clop, clop, clop on the wood. Some of the farmers leaving the gates gave the animal suspicious looks.

The men at the city gates wore unfamiliar uniforms, but their faces were undeniably Saarlander.

One called, "Halt! Who enters the city?"

"We be wanting to sell cabbages," Loesie said. "Also, we found someone's horse jus' wandering around. It don't look like a farm horse."

The guard eyed the horse and the thistles stuck in the fetlocks. "No, that don't look like a farm horse."

He walked around the group, stopping to examine Johan Delacoeur. "Stole yesself a nice jacket, huh?"

Johan's face went red, but to his credit, he said nothing.

The guard eyed Martine, who held her chin up and glared back at him. Calling him a traitor would be unhelpful, but she looked like she very much wanted to.

Then he turned to Johanna. She studied the man's face, hard and unemotional. It occurred to her that it might not be his choice to work for Alexandre. Johanna wondered if, facing the same situation, she would be strong enough to stand up to the occupying army, especially if they were threatening her family. Ultimately, life was about survival, and there was no point in picking fights you couldn't hope to win.

The guard snorted and shifted his attention to Roald, who had pulled his hat over his forehead so that people wouldn't see his face. Fortunately, few Saarlanders knew him by sight, and the guard was not one of those people.

Meanwhile, the other guard looked in the wheelbarrow that Loesie had put down. "Harvest hasn't been the best, huh?"

"No, sir," Nellie said. "But we sell what we can spare so's we can buy blankets for the winter." She sounded quite convincing. If anything, Nellie had constantly surprised Johanna with her strength. Only one thing upset her badly: unwanted advances from a man.

The guard snorted.

"All right, into town with you. Excuses about the questions. There's been too many strange characters entering here today."

They started walking again. Johanna's heart was thudding. Strange characters? What had the guards done with those strange characters?

Johan Delacoeur was muttering under his breath. "What does he think he is, suggesting that I *stole* the jacket. This jacket's mine, sir. I paid for it with my own money, and it was made by a clothes maker many times older and wiser than you—"

"Shh," his wife said. "We're inside, that what matters."

"Well, I'll be sending a complaint to—"

"We're inside. Now be quiet."

It seemed that she was the only person who could shut him up, because he did just that, even though he still didn't look happy.

The scouts Dirk and Jan had been right about the lack of damage in this part of town. Nothing much seemed to have changed here. There were normal people in the streets doing normal things and the houses in this part of the city were undamaged.

But guards were on every street corner, keeping an eye on every passerby. People walked past them, not looking at the men. Johanna felt like she and her group had a big sign over their head. She kept wanting to pull the hat further over Roald's face. She hoped the guards had more attention for the horse than for who held the rope, or that they were more interested in Loesie, who didn't look normal at the best of times.

Johan Delacoeur and his wife walked arm in arm behind the others and didn't draw quite as much attention from the guards.

"They're looking at us," Roald said.

"Yes, I know. Just don't look back."

"I don't want them to look at us."

"I can't help that." As soon as she said this, Johanna knew she had made a mistake.

Roald burst out, "I don't want them to!"

The horse sidestepped and tossed its head.

"Shhh!"

Roald's eyes were wide and his breaths were fast. He wasn't going to have a screaming fit, was he? He'd been really tense all day. Heart thudding, she took his hand and placed it on the horse's neck. She pressed his fingers into the warm fur, scratching the horse with him. His skin was sweaty.

She spoke to him in a low voice. "Calm down. Don't look at anyone, don't listen to anyone, don't speak."

He nodded, still looking at the horse.

They continued, slowly at first, but they sped up when Roald calmed. But now Johanna grew nervous. The further into town they went, the more likely it was that someone would recognise her. What would she say?

Next to Johanna, Loesie was looking so much over her

shoulder that she bumped the wheelbarrow into a woman carrying a basket.

The woman gave a little squeal and dropped the basket on top of the cabbages in the wheelbarrow. "Oh, watch where you're going with that thing." She was a merchant wife or domestic servant, sturdy, broad, with healthy red cheeks.

"Why blame me? You should watch where you're walking." Loesie picked up the basket and shoved it in the woman's hands.

Her face went red. "You rude little—"

Johan Delacoeur joined the group, and Johanna intervened before he could start with his *Do you know who I am?* tone. "We're very sorry that my friend bumped into you. It's our first time coming to the markets. Which way to go?"

The woman jerked her head. "That way. But if you're going to be this rude, you won't sell much."

She gave Loesie a glare and hurried along.

Johanna had been about to say something to Loesie about not creating a fuss, but closed her mouth again. An expression of horror had come over Loesie's face.

"Anything wrong?" Johanna asked.

"I touched the basket. That's why I ran into her. I saw the basket. I wanted to see what it could tell me."

By the Triune, that was a smart thing to do. Johanna should have thought of doing that herself.

"And? What did you see?"

"A lot of scared people. The usurper lives in a house at the markets. People line up in front of his door begging for him to give them food and clothes. He comes out, wearing pretty clothes, and walks straight past them. There is a man with him, with long dark hair. He also dresses pretty. I've seen him before."

"Octavio Nieland?"

"I don't know who that is."

Johanna forgot that Loesie had only come here to sell cheese and baskets.

Loesie continued, "The men walk across the markets. They're laughing. They're not paying any attention to the poor woman with the bandages on her face. Then Alexandre turns around and sets fire to her. Her clothes catch fire. She screams and rolls around on the ground, but no one helps her. That's what I'm seeing."

"No one helps her?"

Loesie shook her head. "People walk past, but no one stops. People are scared."

Johan Delacoeur said, "Much has changed, even if most of it is invisible."

"I don't like it," his wife said.

No, Johanna didn't like it either. If people were this scared, would they still support the royal family?

CHAPTER 5

GRADUALLY, THE STREETS changed. First they came across sections of paving that had been dug up. Loesie had some trouble pushing the wheelbarrow across and Johanna and Nellie had to help her. Roald took care to guide the horse, and Johan Delacoeur wanted to guide his wife by the arm, but she retorted that she had just spent months navigating a slippery riverbank to get water and do washing, and she was capable of walking herself. At which he muttered something about not having married a fishwife.

Johanna laughed secretly at hearing this exchange. Yes, she liked Martine Delacoeur.

Fences had been removed along both sides of the road. Some houses looked abandoned, and people had removed doors and windows, presumably because they were needed elsewhere.

A bit later, they came past the first houses that showed signs of fire damage, mostly boarded-up windows and peeling paint on doors and window frames.

"Look, there," Nellie said.

A house across the street had lost part of its roof. Blackened beams stuck into the sky. As the scouts had said, the pattern of damage was strange. It had skipped certain houses while affecting others.

There was a gasp from behind. Johanna looked over her shoulder. Martine Delacoeur stopped in the middle of the street. She covered her mouth with her hands, staring into a side street. Johan's face was unreadable, perhaps a bit paler than usual.

"Your house?" Johanna asked.

She nodded.

"Burnt?"

"No. I don't think so." She walked into the street, first slowly and then faster.

Johanna followed, telling Roald, Loesie and Nellie to wait. She sort-of knew where the Delacoeurs lived, but didn't remember the exact house.

Martine squealed and started running, while Johan followed, muttering. His wife ran up the steps of a house on the right hand side of the street. The house had some broken windows but was mostly still intact.

She tried to open the door, but it was locked. Then she banged on the door. "Lotta, Lotta, we're back!"

After a little while, the door opened and the woman who stood in the opening was obviously not Lotta, because Johanna knew Lotta, a cousin of Nellie's, and this woman was much older than that.

"Well . . ." She looked taken aback.

"What are you doing in our house?" Johan blustered.

"Well . . . I . . ." Her cheeks went red. "We got the house fair and square. It was abandoned."

"Who said you could live here?"

"The house was empty—"

"Because we had to run for our lives. The house was not yours to take."

"The Town Council said—"

"Which Town Council? The one that includes the man who burnt all this down?"

"Well, I . . ."

A man came into the hallway behind her. "Why are you bothering my wife?"

"Bothering? Bothering?" Johan's face had gone red. "You're in my house, that's what."

The man gave him a hard stare. "You're a liar. The real Johan Delacoeur would never go around dressed up in dirty clothing like that. Go away, man, you're nothing but a simple peasant. In any case, if you really wish to complain, I recommend that you take it up with the regent. He decreed that we need to share available housing."

"The regent . . ." Johan's face grew even redder. "Let me tell you what I think of this *regent*—"

Martine pulled his sleeve. "Shh, darling calm down. We don't want too much trouble."

He whirled around at her. "Trouble? He's in our house and you talk about *trouble*?"

"Just calm down," Martine said. "Guards are coming this way."

"Guards? This is ridiculous. I'll tell them who we are—"

"Come, Johan." She pulled him away from the door, which shut.

"I don't understand you, woman. First we had to come here dressed up like this, then you don't want me to throw these people out of our house. I'll—"

"We'll get them out later. Let's not create a fuss straight away. Think of keeping the king safe."

Johan snorted, but returned to the place where Roald, Loesie and Nellie were, even if he was grumbling and red-faced. Johanna thought she could see tears in Martine's eyes. And so the Delacoeurs were the first people who found themselves homeless. And Martine was right in that they could absolutely not afford a fuss. Probably, too, if many houses had been burnt, there would have been a shortage and of course empty houses would be used if there was no sign of the original owners. Martine suggested that they go to check on her sister's, so the pair of them went off in another direction.

Johanna watched them go with growing apprehension. If the time came, would Johan help her or would he side with the nobles in power? That was the big question. She thought the common people would support her, but without support of at least some nobles, Roald might as well walk to the jail straight away.

She pushed that thought away. "Let's go to the markets first." Get rid of that horse and the wheelbarrow, and then check what was left of her house.

Johanna didn't like the look on Roald's face. He was staring at his feet, and his lips were twitching.

She went to walk next to him, but didn't dare touch him because that would draw attention. She spoke softly. "We're going to take the horse to the barn and then we're going to my house." If there was still a house to go to.

He didn't reply or react, so she asked, "Are you all right?"

He nodded, stiffly. She didn't think he was all right. He should really be off the street, and soon.

They were now coming to the more badly affected part of town. Several houses along the street were so badly burnt that they were uninhabitable, but houses next door had remained untouched. It was really strange. The smell of fire hung in the street. One fire was smouldering, with wisps of smoke drifting into the street.

"They're still burning houses," Nellie said in a soft voice. Her face had gone white. Her family lived two blocks from here. They should go to check on them, too.

Loesie nodded, still hugging herself.

In the next street, two more houses were burned, also in haphazard fashion. A guard stood in front of one of those houses. Next to him sat a bear on its rump with the forepaws resting on the ground.

The accompanying guard was not a Saarlander. He had dark hair, which he wore loose over his cloak. He stood still, only his eyes moving, following the group down the street.

Whether it was the clopping of the horse's hooves or a foreign smell on the wind, Johanna didn't know, but the bear grunted and heaved itself on all its four paws.

The horse shied and pulled at the reins. Parts of the whites were showing in its eyes.

"Shh." Roald patted the animal's neck. Johanna grabbed the end of the rope, briefly touching Roald's hands. They were clammy and sweaty.

The guard gave the group a penetrating look, as if he knew exactly who they were.

Johanna's heart thudded like crazy. She didn't dare look over her shoulder, but she suspected that he would use a pigeon or some magical thing to warn Alexandre. *Oh, look, the lost prince has been found. He's coming in your direction. Half a dozen soldiers should take care of him.*

She had to force herself to abandon that line of thought.

Closer to the markets, the fire damage became more

prominent. Large swathes of houses had been burned, whole streets turned into a wasteland of blackened stone walls and skeleton-like remains of floors and roofs. Nothing was smouldering here.

There were some signs that people were rebuilding, with stacks of bricks and planks of wood, but many ruins lay abandoned, with weeds growing in the formerly neat yards. Where were the people? Wasn't this the street where Master Willems lived? Used to live, she thought with a chill. There was no way he would have survived if he had been home.

The markets were at the end of the street; and it was quite busy here, with people making their way across the blackened ground carrying produce. None of them took any notice of a man in a grey cloak who kneeled on the ground at one of the ruins.

There used to be a small church in that spot, the precursor of the large church in the market place. The grey-cloaked figure buried his face in his hands. Of course it was the Shepherd Carolus and Johanna guessed that the church had been his.

Johanna wanted to go comfort him, but couldn't. They were not supposed to know each other.

Another guard with a bear came into the street walking towards the group. The man noticed the Shepherd and before anyone could do anything, belted Shepherd Carolus from behind. He fell face down in the soot. Johanna stood frozen. What could she do? Help him and risk Roald, or let the Shepherd suffer?

She knew Carolus wouldn't want her to risk herself, but still she couldn't just leave him there. He might be badly hurt. But then he heaved himself onto his hands and knees, coughing. Johanna followed the others to the markets, staring ahead as if she saw things like this every day. Inside, she was crying.

They rounded the street corner and came to the markets. Johanna almost gasped.

Not only was the church gone, but the houses on one side of the marketplace were gone, too. You could see across the area of soot and rubble to the canal that ran at the back of those houses. The grocery store, the inn, the barbershop, the candlemaker's shop were all gone.

The land where the church had stood had been cleared.

Two workers were digging trenches in the muddy ground marked with pegs and pieces of string. It looked like they were building a new large construction, but their toil in the mud resembled a punishment more than it did a real building site.

The roof to the market and weigh house had sagged inwards and the normally open sides had been boarded up. Someone had constructed a new set of weighing scales for market produce, and a roof to protect it from the weather, all of it made out of rubble, but it was a poor construction, nowhere near as solid and pretty as the old weigh house.

The houses on the far side of the markets had mostly survived. They belonged to rich families, were built mostly from stone and had sustained minor damage at the most.

As the two scouts had said, a long row of common citizens waited in front of the undamaged mayor's house. The start of the queue was kept at the bottom of the steps by a pair of long-haired guards in bearskin cloaks. Most of the people in the queue wore several layers of coats and blankets, and some had brought fold-up stools as if knowing they'd stand in that queue all day. Johanna didn't want to stare at them too much, for fear of being recognised.

The curtains were open at the ground floor of the house, and Johanna could see movement inside. Had Alexandre brought a wife and family here?

As for the markets: the meagre number of stalls that occupied the middle of the soot-stained paving was a pale shade of the vibrancy of the marketplace before the fires. Many of the vendors used to come from outside town, and those people would be too scared to come—or dead.

Nellie and Loesie—with the wheelbarrow—led the way between the stalls and Johanna followed with Roald and the horse, eying the miserable produce for sale. Cabbages and worm-ridden apples everywhere. There were also some potatoes, eggs, carrots and parsnips, but the harvest must have been poor, and if this was going to be enough to feed the people of Saardam then by the Triune, there weren't many people left.

Father.

A chill went through her at the thought of crossing the markets, going to her house to find out the ultimate truth. Which might be joyful, but it could also be really, really terrible. The fact that she was about to find out made her feel ill.

Someone called, "Mistress Johanna!"

Underneath the cover of a stall stood a familiar person: Leo Mustermans, the cheese seller whom she used to visit.

Johanna ran to the stall. "Shh."

He came out from behind the stall and swept her up in a hug. "We all thought you were dead, with the palace burnt down and the *Lady Sara* stolen." He was a lot less chubby than he used to be, and with the fat gone from his cheeks, he looked to have aged ten years. "Oh, look at you!"

"We took the *Lady Sara* to safety."

"And you come back disguised as farmers."

"It's a very long story, but we're hoping that there are still people here who support the royal family."

"You will find plenty. They're battered and bruised and scared, but there are plenty. You do know that the king and queen were both killed, right?"

"I do. But did anyone ever tell you that the crown prince was dead, too?"

"They did. They said he drowned in the harbour and that was why there is no body."

"They were lying. The prince is a very good swimmer."

Leo patted the horse and then met Roald's eyes. His eyes went wide. "Is that. . . ?"

"Oh, you haven't met my husband?"

He gasped. His face went red and he held his hand over his mouth to stop shouting his excitement. But a couple of people around him noticed his reaction and looked at Johanna.

A man said, "Why, that's Miss Brouwer. I'd heard people say that she was dead."

"No, no," his wife said. "Look at the young man."

Roald's face went pale. He let go of the horse's rope. Johanna managed to grab it just in time before the horse could create trouble and draw the attention of the guards.

"Look after the horse," she whispered to him, rather more sharply than she normally would have.

"I don't want to talk to people." It sounded like his teeth were chattering.

"You don't have to. Hold the horse. Let me do the talking."

"It's the prince!" someone called.

"The prince is back."

"The Triune be praised!" said a merchant.

His wife berated him. "Shush and don't say that. Do you want your house burned like Master Pieters?"

More people ran closer to have a look.

Johanna stepped forward so that Roald stood between her and the horse. There were at least twenty people facing her, mostly merchants. Nellie had come to stand next to her. Johanna's back touched Roald's side. He was swaying, the muscles under his sleeves tensing.

"We're farmers selling our produce, and we want to sell a horse." She spoke in a loud voice. Her heart was thudding. Any moment now and the guards would notice the gathering, or Roald would go into panic mode and then they would definitely notice him.

Several people nodded and dropped off. They understood.

"If you want to buy a horse, let this man here know about it." She indicated Leo the cheese seller.

Further nods.

"I'd like to put a bid on that horse," said a man.

Others made agreeing noises. They assured Leo that he'd be hearing from them and went back to their stalls.

"That was a smart thing to do," Leo said.

"I'm sorry about drawing you into this—"

"I'd be honoured, lady. I happen to have become a horse seller today. Except that looks like a coach horse. You could be in trouble for trying to sell it."

"We found it wandering around outside the city walls. I'm not sure what we should do with it. Roald wants to keep it. He likes horses."

"I'll find a safe stable for it where no one is going to accuse you of stealing."

"Thank you."

"No, thank you. You give us hope."

Johanna didn't know what to say to that. From what she had seen, they needed a whole lot more than just hope.

"We're going to see my house now. Is my father all right?"

"Alive. Don't know about all right, but he's alive."

Johanna breathed out a sigh of relief. "And the house?"

"Still standing." He hesitated. He eyed Roald again. Roald was scratching the horse's ears and the horse was nuzzling his clothes. Roald really did have an extraordinary way with animals.

"Your husband, right?"

"We've shared the bed since the day we arrived in Aroden for help, but found that Aroden had been burned to the ground."

His eyes went wide. "Oh, we'd hoped they would help us, if only we could send out someone to tell them."

"There won't be any help from Aroden. It's up to us."

Then he looked at Johanna and bowed. "Your Majesty. It would be an honour to serve you."

"Shhh. Nothing is official, and if anyone asks, you didn't see us here."

"You're right. I didn't see anyone I haven't met yesterday."

CHAPTER 6

LEO SAID IT WAS no more risky to go to her house than to walk anywhere else. "Which is pretty risky, mind. Those magicians are everywhere, and they know everything. Including about horses. They'll have seen you come in with this animal and they'll want to know what you've done with it. You be very, very careful."

"What about you?"

"I have my way of solving these problems, lady."

They left him to look after the horse and the produce they had brought, and continued to the other side of the markets. The fire had also hit hard here, but had spared pockets of houses. In one such pocket Johanna found her own house. Some of the windows had broken from the heat, and paint had peeled off, but the steps were clean and swept and a glow of light came from within Father's library.

The door was bolted from inside and when Johanna let the knocker fall, quick footsteps approached.

The door first opened a crack. An eye peeked out.

43

"Koby?" At least Johanna thought it was Koby.

A squeal; then the door opened further. Definitely Koby.

"Mistress Johanna! Quick, come in, come in!"

Johanna went up the steps and was enveloped in a gravy-scented hug.

"Come and look at this, master, Johanna is back!"

The door to the library opened and there was Father. Greyer than she remembered him, and leaning on a walking stick. He wore his favourite jacket but had lost so much weight that it hung off his shoulders like a sack. But he was alive.

Johanna extricated herself from Koby's arms and hugged him tightly. His shoulders were so thin that she could feel the bones through his jacket. His grip was so feeble that she thought her hug would break him.

For a while he could say nothing except, "Oh, oh, oh." Then he recovered a bit. "We thought you were lost. When I couldn't find you in the burning palace . . ." Tears rolled over his cheeks.

Then he looked past her to the others who had come into the hall, where Koby had once again bolted the door.

"Nellie has become a good lady, too, I see, and who is the other young lady?"

"That's Loesie."

"Your basket-selling friend?"

"Yes." She was surprised that he remembered her.

"And the young man?"

"That's a bit of a story. We fled in the *Lady Sara*. Loesie knew how to handle the sea cows. We went upriver to find help, but all we saw along the river was destruction and death. Aroden castle is completely burnt. There is nothing left, so we thought we were the only Saarlanders left—"

"Wait, you said the *Lady Sara*?"

"Yes. It's moored around the river bend just outside the city gates."

"The *Lady Sara* has survived?"

"There might be a small scratch on it somewhere, and we lived in the hold and modified it into a room, but yes—"

"Oh, heavens be praised! I thought I'd lost everything. The *Lady Davida* was burned in the fire and I thought the Brouwer Company was doomed after all the work I put into it my entire life. Oh, you can't possibly understand how happy I am that you're back—" He frowned at Roald. "I think I know who you are, but . . . it can't be. They said you'd drowned."

"King Roald of Saarland," Johanna said.

"Oh," was the only thing he said before he dropped into a stiff bow.

Roald froze. He never seemed to know what to do in situations like this.

I must teach him, Johanna thought. "Come on, Father, that's not necessary. We've travelled with him for months. We need a safe place to stay. He's my husband."

Now Father looked up, his eyes wide. "You . . . Oh, heavens be praised! I thought I'd lost everything. My wife, my daughter, my first and dearest ship." Tears were streaming down his face. "And on top of that . . . you're saying that you married the prince."

"I did. Nellie did the service when we thought that everyone was lost and we couldn't get help at Aroden. It's not official, but it's the most official we could make it."

"Oh, what a day, what a day. There is hope yet for all of us. You must stay here. We have plenty of room in the house. I'll see to it that you get the best room, and that it's clean and that there are fresh sheets and clean clothes. We lost some of our workers. Jan was killed trying to put out the fires." Jan used to look after the garden and fix things in the house. "Adrian went down with the *Lady Davida*. She is still in the place where she sank, burned and all, at the bottom of the harbour. We never found Adrian. And the Hendricksen warehouse burned down. The old man died a few weeks later from the burns. His poor widow has been living in poverty ever since. And so many people have left town. Your family, too, Nellie."

Nellie's eyes widened. "They're alive?"

Johanna felt guilty that she hadn't yet walked past Nellie's house.

"As far as I know, they are, but the house is lost, so they had nowhere to live. They were involved with the church, too. This filth has been punishing people from the Church of the Triune for something they didn't do. You know I was never keen on that church, but they didn't cause the fires. The church did nothing wrong. But far too many people believe what this terrible man says, many of them nobles—"

"Octavio Nieland."

"Yes, he, and many of the other nobles. Alexandre gives them the influence they always wanted and King Nicholaos was unwilling to give them—" He bowed to Roald. "I'm very sorry about your parents, Your Majesty. We will protect you against these evil men."

It was disturbing how he had gone from being a confident man to one hoping for miracles. "You have to tell me about everything that happened here."

"Yes, yes, but first you must hide."

"We're already hidden. We're off the street, the door is shut and—"

Someone dropped the knocker on the wood.

There was a moment of intense silence. Father's eyes widened as he turned to the door, a horrified expression on his face. He put his finger to his lips.

"You must hide *now*," he whispered. "Quick, go upstairs and be very quiet. Don't speak. They must not see you here. They must not hear you."

All right. "Come," Johanna whispered to the others. She led Nellie, Loesie and Roald to the stairs and, on the landing between the two floors, went through the little door that led into the storeroom above Father's office.

"Be very quiet now," she said.

Whereas before the storeroom had been full of spare dinner things, now the room contained a lot of Father's nice dinnerware and the precious treasures brought from other lands during his travels. Why weren't those things in the cabinets in the sitting room anymore?

CHAPTER 7

THEY SAT DOWN on the floor, while in the hallway downstairs, Koby pulled back the bolts that held the door shut.

"No, no," she was saying. "I was just talking to the master. He's in the library waiting for you."

Someone replied, the voice too soft to recognise or make out words.

"What are we doing here?" Roald asked in a too-loud voice. "Hiding? I like playing hide and seek."

"Shh. It's a game. Be very, very quiet now."

He nodded. "I like playing hide and seek. You know I used to play it with—"

"Shhh!"

He giggled, but covered his mouth with his hand so he didn't make any noise.

Like this, he looked like an overgrown child, his eyes bright, innocent to the terrible things people did to each other. She loved him for that simple, unconditional attention that he gave her. Nellie had her lips pursed. Johanna knew that she disapproved of listening to conversations.

Loesie lay on her stomach in front of the window, looking into the garden.

Downstairs, the door to Father's library opened and the person, or persons, came inside the hall with the clack-clacking of high-heeled boots on the marble floor, and then the more muffled sound as the visitor walked onto the carpet.

"Good morning, Dirk." It was a dry, male voice that Johanna didn't recognise. One of the proper nobility, judging by the cultured sound of his speech. "It's a very good morning, don't you think?"

"Never since the light of my life was taken from me has there been a good morning."

Whoa, since when did Father speak like that?

There was the sound of a chair being dragged across the mat. "Suit yourself, Dirk. I've brought the contract for signing."

A period of silence. Johanna pictured a man putting a piece of paper on Father's desk.

"What, Dirk, are you not going to sign it?"

And pictured Father pushing the paper back across the desk.

"I would like some time to think about it." She pictured Father giving the man his famous critical look. A glimmer of hope sparked in her that his famous sense of business had not been damaged too much.

"Even more time than you've already had? You're not getting any younger. You might drop dead tomorrow, and then who is going to inherit your wealth? Who is going to run your business?" The arrogant tone of the voice was starting to annoy her. Who was this upstart?

The arrogant voice continued, "Are you going to ruin

the life of my sister as well as the lives of your wife and daughter?"

"You vile snake!"

The man laughed. "You can call me whatever you want. The fact is my sister is the only one who has volunteered to share an old man's bed to beget him another heir. And getting heirs was never your strong point, Dirk."

"Shut. Up! Before I wring your skinny neck."

Again that dry laugh. "You're welcome to try. But you're an old man, Dirk, and you know that. This is your last chance. All right, then. I'm reasonable. Have your few days to *think about it*. I'm patient. Lisbeth is patient. You will die long before she. I'll leave you with this document. Just have your secretary bring it up to my office when you've changed your mind." The chair was dragged over the carpet. "Oh, I forgot. Your secretary has been missing."

One more chuckle and he left the room.

The door creaked. High-heeled boots hit the floor in the hall. Koby said something, but her voice was too soft for them to hear what. The man replied, "No, that's not necessary." The front door opened and shut.

Koby dragged the bolt across.

That was when Johanna first dared move.

Lisbeth? Lisbeth LaFontaine? A young woman a few years older than Johanna, a cousin of Fleuris LaFontaine. Hadn't she been married last year? Hadn't her husband died soon after?

And by the missing secretary, did he mean Master Willems?

She met Nellie's eyes, and Nellie, having heard everything, stared back, a puzzled look on her face. "What in the Triune's name is happening in this town?"

Loesie turned to them. "It's the hand of evil."

Johanna swore that there was a haze of white in her eyes when she said that. She shuddered.

She left the storeroom, followed by Roald, Nellie and Loesie. Nellie and Loesie were short enough to be able to walk under the beams, but Roald hit his head twice.

Johanna shielded his head from the last beam, and when she touched the wood, saw some men carrying boxes full of Father's pretty treasures from the sitting room through the little doorway and up the stairs. Johanna recognised the men. They were porters who used to work in the warehouse.

One of the men said, "If they search the house, they'll find all these things."

"The trick is not to let anyone know that this is here, so they won't search for it."

This had to have happened a few days after the fire. Maybe Alexandre's bandits were looting the town. Maybe the council had asked for citizens to hand in their wealth.

In the downstairs hall, the door to the library was open. Father sat slumped in his chair and did not look up, even though he must have heard them come down the stairs.

"Look, why don't we go and help in the kitchen?" Nellie said in a low voice to Loesie.

Loesie and Roald trundled after her. Poor Koby.

Johanna went into the room. Father looked up and sighed. "You heard."

"They're forcing you to get married?" It was hard to believe.

He sighed and nodded. "I need an heir. That much is true."

"No you don't. Not anymore. You have your heir." And hopefully, there would be a new generation at some point.

"But he doesn't know that, and he can't be allowed to find out."

Also true. "That was Auguste LaFontaine?" She remembered him as a small man with a thin, sharp face who never had much good to say about other people.

He nodded. "It's his sister Lisbeth whose life they're trying to ruin. I don't believe for one moment that she volunteered."

"But why? Why her? Why don't you just walk away from his silly proposal and tell them to go somewhere else?"

"It's not as simple as that. The *Lady Davida* was lost in the fire and the *Lady Sara* is missing. The LaFontaine family owns the only shipyard in town that survived the fire. They will build me a new boat, but I have to agree to their conditions, otherwise they won't take the order."

"And their conditions are to marry Lisbeth?"

He nodded and looked down. "To make the filthy LaFontaine family the owner of my business, whatever it's still worth." He spread his hands, let them sink to his sides and shrugged. "It will be worth less every day that I don't have a ship." The light from the fire made the wrinkles in his face show up like canyons. "I can't operate a river trading company without a boat."

"But you have the *Lady Sara* again."

"That's why I won't be signing this." He scrunched the document up into a ball and threw it in the fire. Flames quickly turned their prey into an inferno. Within moments, there was nothing left of the paper.

"Won't that get you into trouble?" Johanna asked.

He gave a wry smile. "If it does, it will have been worth

it. I've wanted to do that for a while. Frankly, I think they were disappointed that I didn't die in the fire. People have been looking at me as an example of withstanding the tyrants. But I'm old and tired. I don't know how much longer I could have refused them, and now I don't know how much longer they will stay polite."

"Then we must act quickly."

He held up his hands. "What can we do? There are so few of us and no one wants to risk their family."

"We're going to reclaim our town. We have the rightful king, and we're going to get the people behind us—."

"Reclaim the town? You mean get rid of Alexandre? You can't. Have you seen what he can do? They call him the Fire Wizard. He sets fire to people's houses with a wave of his hand. He's done that to everyone who doesn't agree with him. He'll burn down the whole town before he'll leave."

"I don't think so. He could have burned all of Saardam already if that's what he wants, but I think he wants Saardam reasonably intact—maybe because he needs us as workers, maybe for some other reason. He doesn't want to destroy the town, he wants to control the town."

"That's what tyrants usually want, tormenting poor people to amuse themselves. This man is evil, Johanna, and I don't want you standing up to him, because he will kill you."

"Only you can stand up to him?"

He opened his mouth, spread his hands, closed his mouth again and let his hands fall by his sides. "I just want you to be careful. That's all."

CHAPTER 8

I T WAS TIME for the midday meal, which was being
set on the table by Koby and Nellie, while Roald
fussed about with tableware and finger bowls.

Koby tried to do it for him, but he wouldn't let her. She
apologised, red-cheeked. "Oh, I'm sorry that the prince is
doing this work. I couldn't help it."

"Never mind, Koby. Let him help you if he wants to.
Thank you."

Father sat down and Johanna took her usual place at
the table. Roald looked a bit lost so she waved for him to
sit next to her. Johanna noticed that he had flour on
his hands.

Nellie would once again eat downstairs, even though it
felt strange. "Where is Loesie?"

Koby gave her a sharp look. "You know that girl is a
witch, don't you?"

"Yes, I do. She has helped us for months." *And brought
us into danger*, but she left that unsaid.

"Witches are dangerous. If nothing else, they're spies
from the Belaman Church."

"I assure you, Koby, Loesie is nothing of the sort. She's my friend and she should be here, because with her magic, she will be important in our plans." If, in some way, Johanna could figure out how to get Loesie using her magic.

"As you wish, mistress." Koby left the room.

"Sit down, Roald," Johanna said when the door had closed behind her.

He did, in his usual, nervous, straight-backed manner. Roald and Father looked at each other. Father nodded, perhaps a bit puzzled. People behaved like that around Roald. They didn't quite know what to say, because Roald didn't come across as expecting bows and curtsies and wasn't interested in conversations about trivialities. She would have to work out a way of getting Roald to accept that people wanted to do this, and to get him to react in a way that didn't confuse those people.

She wondered what King Nicholaos and Queen Cygna had done for him, except send him away to the Guentherite brotherhood farm for unruly royals. The memory she had of Roald running after his sister's birthday friends squealing had taken on new meaning. Back then, she'd thought it was fun, but now she understood how distressed he must have been. She put a hand on his knee under the table. The tense muscles in his legs relaxed a little.

"Tell us what has happened here while we were gone," she said to Father.

Father spread the napkin on his lap and took his spoon. His hand shook. He was about to start eating when he stopped and lowered the spoon again.

"They were bad tidings." He scooped up a spoonful of soup. "When I lost you in that hall, the best I could do was try to get home, hoping that you had also made your way there. The whole town was in chaos and people were running for their lives. I found the house undamaged, but you weren't here."

His expression grew distant. "I was too scared to go out again. Bandits with bears were roaming the streets. I'm but an old man and I thought if I went out there and died, you would have no one to come back to. So I chose to be a coward, and hid inside. I also couldn't face sending Koby into that chaos."

He let the soup fall back into the plate. "Many people lost their lives that night. I went out in the morning to look for you. The city was a wasteland. Many houses were still burning. I . . . couldn't find you anywhere. . . ."

He swallowed hard and wiped at his eyes. "Not Master Willems, either. His family's house was gone. The office was still there, but it was damaged, and the sea cow barn had been spared. But the only thing I could see of the *Lady Davida* were the masts sticking out of the water. The bandits and the bears were gone, too, and some people were in the streets trying to help. Octavio Nieland was one of those people. I've never considered him to be helpful, especially not towards common people. But he gave them food, cooked by his housekeeper, even though his own parents and his sister were said to be amongst the people who didn't make it out of the palace."

"Julianna came back with me."

His eyes widened.

"We caught up with her in Florisheim. She and Captain Arense took the *Prosperity* upriver."

"Well, that's . . . good news."

Johanna didn't like the hesitation. "Julianna is all right. You know I never liked her, but she has changed. She was sick, but she came through and has helped me ever since. She knows how Octavio sold himself to the occupiers. She didn't leave immediately after the fires but later, and she left *because* of what Octavio did. Yes, their parents are probably dead."

He nodded, his face drawn. "If we thought the fire was bad, what happened afterwards was even worse. Alexandre and his band of cronies would walk through town proclaiming that he was the king. Whenever people challenged him, asking him where his crown was, he'd just flick his hand at them, and they'd burst into flames. He said he was looking for betrayers, but he seemed to be targeting members of the Church of the Triune and murdering their entire families. The Shepherd Romulus had survived. . . . You know I was never a great supporter of the church, but . . . this was just awful. He had been badly burnt in trying to stop his church burning down. Say whatever you want, but it was a very nice building. The Shepherd begged Alexandre to help the people. Here was this badly wounded man, with blood and gore oozing from his hands and arms, and he was asking help on behalf of *other* people. Then this . . . monster just flicked his hand and set him on fire and he died screaming. *To help him out of his misery*, he said, and then he laughed. Johanna, we must do something so that we won't ever have to see anything like that again." The waning light that came in through the window cast his face in sharp relief. He looked old and tired.

"I've heard that Alexandre gave a speech."

"Yes, he did, a few days after the fire. It was full of hatred for the Church of the Triune and how he was bringing the only true church."

"The Belaman Church."

He nodded.

"Their teachings include magic."

"They do. He was rounding up people in the streets and scouting them out for magic, which, of course, very few of us have. The ones who were found to have some magic, he forced in his service—"

"Master Willems?"

"I don't know. I hope he fled with the many people who left in disgust. They were not seen again."

"Many of them came up the river in the *Prosperity*. Maybe they expected to find an ally in Aroden or Baron Uti, but Aroden is even worse off than Saardam, and all Baron Uti ever did for the refugees was to let them wait for things that he'd promised, but never delivered. He gave them land to camp on, but did nothing else. His son is pure evil." She shuddered. "There are things I've watched him do that I won't even talk about."

Father frowned. "Baron Uti's son who was at the ball? Who danced with you?"

"Yes." She shuddered.

"What is going on in Florisheim?"

"I wish I knew, but only the Baron knows that, and the Guentherite order of the Belaman Church. They're doing all kinds of magic. Digging black rock out of the ground, and making iron. Waking up all sorts of ghosts." That seemed to sum it up. "Florisheim is full of ghosts. They're coming down the river, and they listen to no one except magicians."

"You'll understand that magic isn't very popular with us survivors. I'm almost beginning to agree with that church of yours wanting to ban it. That's me speaking, a merchant, one of those who married into a magical family."

Johanna shook her head. "Banning it is not the answer.

People still have magic, even if it's fairly rare in Saardam. We will need to use magic if we are to get rid of Alexandre."

He met her eyes, the look in them full of concern. "You really think you can do this, don't you?"

"Not me alone." If only she could find someone to help her. The Baroness Viktoriya called Alexandre a little man, but he had obviously struck fear in the heart of the people of Saardam before they could find out that he was little.

"Do you know anything about him?" Father asked. "He did come across the river from Florisheim, didn't he?"

Johanna nodded. "Alexandre Trebuchet is an ex-resident of the Guentherite brotherhood's farm in Burovia across the river from Florisheim," Johanna explained. "A lot of princes spend time on the farm."

"It's said that he's a cousin of King Leopold of Burovia."

"He is, but I don't think that the king has anything to do with this."

"I don't know. I've always heard that Gelre or Burovia didn't like the influence that the Church of the Triune was holding over Saardam. Apparently, Alexandre came under cover on the Burovian ship that brought the prince back."

"What about all the soldiers that Alexandre brought?"

"The ones with the bears? They are Estlander. They dress in woodland gear, but I've heard them talk, and they're Estlander, from just across the border, most of them."

"They're mercenaries?" That was interesting. Johan Delacoeur said that this wasn't done, that a good military campaign did not rely on hired troops. It brought the interesting possibility that these men with their bears could be *bought*, if enough money could be found. And if what Father said was true, and they came from Estland, maybe the name Sara Aroden—Johanna's mother—would mean something to them.

Roald had been sitting through all this while watching silently. Now he said, "I'm not afraid of that man. He is mean to animals."

Father gave him a strange look. "Animals?"

"He whips the horses and I've seen him kick a dog."

Father frowned. "Um . . ." He met Johanna's eyes.

"When Roald was in Burovia, he worked at the farm where Alexandre lived." Johanna patted Roald's hand under the table. It felt sweaty.

"Oh," Father said. "So Your Majesty is familiar with the reasons why this man occupied our city?"

Roald gave him a blank look, but under the table his hand gripped Johanna's. He didn't "do" reasons, at least not ones that required understanding people.

"No one knows what Alexandre wants," Johanna said. Well, the Baron or Kylian would know, but they weren't going to share.

Koby came into the room and Johanna suggested that Roald go upstairs to get changed and freshen up. Koby showed him upstairs, while Johanna went with Father into the library.

"What is actually wrong with him?" Father asked. "He doesn't strike me as dumb, but something is not right."

"He doesn't like people."

Father laughed at this.

"No, I mean, for real. He doesn't know how to talk to people. He's fine with animals, and he knows everything about them and about history and about the Burovian king's family tree, and he knows about birds and frogs and dragons."

"Dragons?" Father laughed. "They're not real."

"That doesn't matter to him. It's written in a book, so it's real to him. You name it, he knows about it. But he's bad at talking to people."

"So, even his stay at the farm hasn't cured him?"

Johanna shook her head, feeling a bit uneasy and even annoyed at the word *cured*. Roald wasn't sick. He was just a bit strange.

"Could he rule?"

"By himself? No. He would probably just ignore everybody and potter about the rose garden every day."

"Does he know that this is all about him?"

"I think he does." But sadly, Roald couldn't do much to help retake Saardam for his family. If anything, he would need to stay inside a lot and he would get bored. There weren't even any ponds to collect frogs here. There was Father's library, of course. Although it mostly held books about strange lands and their spices.

"What are you going to do when your first child is born and is afflicted with the same condition?"

"Roald's father wasn't afflicted with the condition. And neither was Celine."

"King Nicholaos was odd, in the way that he spent all his money on the church. If Alexandre came here to loot the Carmine coffers, he must have been sorely disappointed."

Johanna felt chilled. "I thought you wanted me to marry Roald."

"That was when the king assured me that his son was cured."

Johanna's cheeks flushed with anger. "Father, I think the only thing that was wrong with King Nicholaos was that he truly didn't care about his son. Maybe he was ashamed of him. Well, I'm not ashamed to say that I care for him."

"No, but this does make the situation more difficult."

"Different, not more difficult. We will do the work for Roald. He just takes up the position, and we help him with what he needs to say."

"I hope so, Johanna. It's not a kind of position I would prefer to be in, considering the evil of the man we're facing. He's not going to be polite because Roald is not quite normal or you're a nice girl. I've seen him burn people to death, both men and women. He has no morals and no serious rivals. You would need a magician to defeat him." His eyes met Johanna's, as if he knew that they were lacking in the magician department.

If only Loesie were a bit more cooperative. Johanna understood why she was hesitant to use her magic, but would she still refuse to help if there was no one else? If it meant Alexandre would win?

After Johanna had said goodnight to Father, she went down into the basement to find Loesie.

But Loesie was not at the table in the kitchen. She was not in any of the servants' rooms. Johanna asked Nellie, who sat combing her hair on her bed, but she hadn't seen Loesie since they had shared the meal in the kitchen.

Koby came into the hallway from the laundry, her cheeks red from the cold.

"The witch?" she said when Johanna asked. "She left. She says she knows when she isn't welcome."

"Left?" Where to?

"Yes, out the door."

"Oh, that is nonsense," Johanna said. "She sat at the table at Duke Lothar's castle."

After all this time together, she had to admit that she

still didn't understand why Loesie would go like this. At first she had thought it was because of the spell, but she was beginning to think that this was just Loesie.

Loesie didn't *want* to be included, just so that she could go on complaining that she wasn't included.

Great. Now what?

Then another thought: the sea cow barn. She had told the other people from the *Prosperity* to meet there if any of them found themselves without family and without a home.

Not only should she check the barn for them, but it was probably where Loesie would be. She often used to sleep there when she came to the markets with her grandma, too.

CHAPTER 9

JOHANNA WAS so tired that she felt she could sleep for a week, but she dressed in her outdoor clothes and dragged her weary limbs back into the cold to look for Loesie.

An icy wind had come up that whipped leaves through the street and prised its cold fingers through the gaps in her clothing. Johanna pulled both sides of her cloak together, shivering, wishing she could be inside by the fire.

And yet, despite the destruction and misery that people obviously suffered here, she was glad that she was in Saardam and no longer in a wet field in Florisheim. The combination of rising water and the coming winter would have been utterly miserable. The nosy baroness would have made things worse. Now that she looked back on it, the baroness had been trying to pull Johanna and Roald into her influence. The woman *had* to know at least some of the things that her son was up to.

Now if only she could understand why Loesie kept running away.

The markets lay deserted in the gathering darkness,

the produce sold or brought inside, the stallholders gone home. The only house where there was light behind the windows was the mayor's, but the queues had gone, even if people in those queues had left little markers—a piece of wood or stone with a name scrawled across it—to remind others of their position.

She walked across the open wasteland of the markets, where the cloth covering the few meagre stalls flapped in the squally breeze.

During the day, she hadn't noticed that in one of the side streets so many houses had been destroyed that it offered a view of the palace gates. Curious, Johanna turned into the street.

On the night of the ball, she had gone through the main gate with Father in the coach to line up in the fore-court at the bottom of the palace steps. She remembered all the noble women in pretty dresses tut-tutting about her presence. This was also where, after the ball, she had last seen Octavio Nieland looking for his parents and palace guards corralling people into coaches. Panicked horses. Creatures made out of fire gambolling over the city's roofs. In the dying daylight, there was no sign of the many bodies that had littered the ground. No sign of the broken coaches and the dead horses.

The gates were closed and held shut with a chain. Johanna pushed, but there was a sturdy lock on the chain.

She peered through the bars. Most of the building was made of stone, and stood far enough away from the rest of town to have remained untouched by the inferno that had flattened the houses around it.

To the right, Queen Cygna's rose garden had been desecrated, the wall broken, the statue of the Triune taken away. There were still drag marks over the ground.

At the palace itself, there were signs that repairs were underway. Johanna didn't remember that the doors were blue—in fact, she was sure they used to be carmine red.

Some stacks of new stones stood to the side of the steps, but piles of leaves had collected between them, so clearly Alexandre had put his efforts into other projects.

It's ours.

No matter the state of the palace, Roald should live in it. This building belonged to Roald and this filthy man did not have the right to touch it, not even to paint the doors blue. She and Roald would live in the palace again, and the children would hold parties in the rose garden, *with* the statue of the Triune.

She clutched the bars of the gate until the metal became too cold for her hands. Then she continued through the ruined streets to the harbour.

The Brouwer Company office on the southern end of the quay had sustained limited damage in the fire, but Father had money and people who would work for him and the roof had since been repaired.

All the buildings on the western side of the harbour had not been so lucky. Most were no more than soot-stained ruins, barely recognisable shells of their former selves. Stacks of bricks stood on the quay, and the foundations for a couple of walls had been built. By the way the walls surrounded an entire block where there used to be two or three buildings, Johanna judged that this was more than a simple rebuilding of the warehouses that used to stand here. The builders had also taken blocks out of the quay and dug out a mooring area set back from the quay wall. Stacks of stone blocks stood on either side. They had pulled up much of the quay's paving as well. What was going on here?

A pocket of the buildings on the eastern side of the harbour still stood, including, by stroke of luck, the king's armoury. The fact that it hadn't exploded was probably responsible for the relatively high survival rate of buildings in this area.

The Brouwer Company's sea-cow barn, two warehouses down from the armoury, had also been spared most of the destruction. Some of the roof tiles had come off and lay haphazardly on the lower roof. One of the doors had blown off its hinges and the other had a big burnt patch in one corner. The roof would leak and the weather would have played havoc with the harnesses and tools stored inside, but the main building was still intact. Without either the *Lady Sara* or *Lady Davida* moored in front, it looked empty.

Johanna walked quickly along the quay and remembered the warehouse next to the barn where she had seen the mysterious men on the evening before the fire.

It was completely empty. Untouched by fire, and empty.

She wasn't sure what to make of that. Who would have had time and ships to empty an entire warehouse after a disaster? What had been in it that needed to be taken away?

A couple of people stood in front of the sea cow barn, huddling in their cloaks.

These were the people from the *Prosperity* who had returned to their houses and found them destroyed and had no other place to go.

She half-expected the Delacoeurs to be there, but they must have found room at Martine's sister's house.

The refugees were a few young men, and Julianna

Nieland, who called out, "There she is!" when Johanna came closer.

"Oh, Julianna!"

Johanna took her hands. They were icy cold.

"I can't go back to my brother," Julianna cried. "I can't stay with any of my family because they will tell him. They're all afraid of him, and I know he makes them do awful things. I don't know what to do. I truly don't."

"I think you should all go back to the *Lady Sara*," Johanna said.

One of the men spoke up. "We most certainly will not, lady. We will stay here with you and fight."

"But we're not fighting anything yet. What use are you going to be when you're cold, hungry and ill? It's almost winter and houses are scarce. You can't sleep here." They could, possibly, sleep in her house. There were several rooms in the attic as well as downstairs in the servants' quarters that were not in use. Julianna could, at the very least, sleep in the spare room on the top floor.

But the LaFontaine family might drop in and find out about these houseguests, and that would be terrible for all concerned. "For now, it would be best if you went back to the *Prosperity,* at least for tonight."

"In the dark?" one of the men said. His name was Jakob, Johanna remembered, and he was the son of a baker.

"The most important thing is that no one discovers that we're back." But she felt horrible about her own safe house and nice bed. "You can sleep in the barn." But the roof leaked.

"I know a better place where we can stay for the night," another young man said. "It will smell of horses, but it will be dry."

That was likely to be in the east harbour, where the newer warehouses stood. There was a horse stable in that area. She nodded agreement. "I'll send someone if we have something better for you."

They said that they would wait, but as the group walked down the quay, Julianna looked so forlorn that Johanna resolved to find a place for her as soon as she could.

She went inside the barn. It took a while for her eyes to get used to the intense darkness, but a crawling sensation crept over her skin. There was magic in the air. She had felt it when coming into town, too. Since when could she feel the presence of magic?

When her eyes had adjusted to the darkness, she found Loesie, as expected, huddled in her usual spot under the tool bench. She had found a disgusting blanket and had lit a small fire in a fire pot that definitely didn't belong to Johanna's father.

Loesie said nothing and Johanna sat down in the straw next to her. The ground was slightly damp, courtesy of the hole in the roof. The air smelled of stale smoke. It was strange to see the water so still, without the occasional snort or flipper from the sea cows breaking the surface. She hoped that the animals belonging in the *Lady Davida's* team had been able to get away and had returned to their wild lives in the ocean.

Loesie came to sit next to her, silent and ghostlike. She was not as thin as she had been when they arrived at Duke Lothar's castle, but still didn't look healthy.

"What are you doing here? Why did you disappear?"

"You know I've always said that I don't belong with all the finery and the pretty houses and pretty dresses."

"But you're my friend. You were with us in the duke's castle. You sat at his table."

"Yes, but I had no choice. I don't like all the pretty things. I'm not pretty and all that stuff makes me nervous."

Yes, Loesie was right. She had always been like this. She loved to point out that she was different. She enjoyed being called a witch and scaring boys. That was why Johanna liked her. Maybe she should just accept it. "At least stay here and come to the house for decent meals."

"That cook doesn't like me."

No, Koby didn't, and Johanna understood why, but still didn't like it. "We'll get the roof fixed for you." It was a lame promise because there was so much that needed doing first, and Loesie continued to say nothing.

Johanna wished she could bring back Loesie's family. She used to talk about "my ma" and laughed at her mother who was silly and didn't know anything about magic. Similarly with Annette, the girl who lived next door and who, according to Loesie, was easily impressed, very girly and gullible. Loesie poked fun at them. The neighbours weren't family, but up there in the little pocket of land where the Rede River branched off from the Saar River, they might as well be, because there were no other farms for miles.

And Loesie was sad and lonely. She could no longer use her magic for fun because magic had suddenly become dangerous, and she wasn't suited to playing games of influence and power.

Johanna didn't know how to help her.

She was about to get up when Loesie said, "It was really kind of you to take me all the way up the river. I got to see a castle and wear fancy dresses and see real magic." Never mind that it hadn't been a leisurely trip and it was not as if they'd had any choice. "You're one of the few people who are decent to me and you've done for me what I don't deserve."

"I think you do. I think you're lonely and you want people around you more than you let out." And it must be terrible for her to have lost her entire family.

"No, I don't."

The intensity in her expression chilled Johanna. She shivered and clamped her arms around herself.

"When I came to the markets that day, I knew that this was about to happen. Well, not exactly this, but I knew that something was going to happen. I knew that the baron's son was behind it. I saw him crossing the river on a water horse. He came to the farm and bought dinner from my grandpa. The neighbour's daughter Annette fancied him. I was jealous and tried to scare her. But he . . . did bad things to her."

"Did you see that?"

"The wood told me. Annette was a beautiful untouched young woman. He threw her in the grass and defiled her. You remember that woman's scream you heard in the basket I gave you? That was her voice. When he finished with her, and she lay broken and crying in the mud, he changed her into a tree, and then he tried to do the same with me. He only kissed me, he didn't do any of the other stuff he did to Annette. But the kiss took my voice right away. And he changed my family into trees, too. He said I had to stay on the farm, but I got some magic on me, so I got away. The spell he put on me was with me the whole way."

"The only thing he did was kiss you?" Johanna felt sick.

"Yes. Proper kissing, on the mouth."

"Did you feel anything after he did that?"

Loesie gave her a wide-eyed look. "Well, yeah. I was jealous of Annette, because he fancied her. He was the biggest spunk that had ever set foot on our farm, so when he came up and kissed me, I felt all sorts of things that city folk say is inappropriate for a woman to feel. But he could have ripped the clothes off me and I wouldn't have said a peep."

The blood rose to Johanna's cheeks. She didn't quite ask for that frank an admission. "I meant did you feel the spell when he kissed you?"

By the Triune, could *she* have been betraying Roald from the moment she left the palace? Was that how Sylvan had known where she was? Hadn't he said something about feeling magic in the air? She'd thought he was talking about Loesie.

"Only that I couldn't speak. All the other stuff, like that I had fits, only came later."

Johanna's stomach roiled.

She tried to remember the night that she'd had dinner with Kylian in the Guentherite farmhouse. She had seen him try to perform necromancy. Why hadn't she refused his hospitality? What actually happened after dinner? And why didn't she remember? Had he kissed her again? Had he done "other things"?

Loesie continued, but Johanna only heard her through the roaring of blood in her ears. "While we were travelling, the spell he had put on me was getting worse and worse. Then we got to the duke's castle and he and you broke the spell but I still couldn't tell you. Every time I wanted to, I thought of something else. Because part of him was still inside me. Still is. That's why I can't sleep in your pretty house with your nice family. That's why I don't want to have anything to do with magic, and why I can't be your court magician. Why I tried to kill myself. I'm afraid I'll betray you. Maybe I already have."

"You said *part of him is inside me*. What do you mean? Did he . . . did he make you with child?"

"No. I said, far as I know, he didn't touch me in that way."

As far as you know? Johanna nodded, trying to look merely interested, trying her best to swallow down sickness. "Why can you tell me only now?"

"I don't know. Maybe we're far enough away from him that he doesn't have influence over me anymore. Maybe something else has changed. Maybe now that you're here close to his friend the Fire Wizard, he doesn't need me anymore."

All of a sudden Johanna could no longer listen or sit still. She ran out of the barn. Stood on the quay not knowing where to go or what to do. Her stomach roiled. She was dizzy. Her mouth flooded with saliva. She was going to be sick, or faint, or both.

Be sick first. She dropped to her knees and vomited, with great gasps. Again and again until there was nothing left inside her, but she dry-retched and couldn't breathe. She saw black spots in her vision. She was going to die.

"That's how it started with me, too," Loesie commented behind her.

Well, that's very helpful, thanks.

Johanna felt better after that. Come to think of it, she'd felt a bit off the last few days. She had probably caught something.

CHAPTER 10

JOHANNA WALKED home in the dark. She didn't see any guards, but there were some people in the street in front of the house so she felt her way through the back yard and came into the entrance to the back of the house. Koby sat in the kitchen, talking to a young man who had to be the new groundsman.

Koby's eyes widened. "Oh my goodness, Mistress Johanna, what have you done to yourself?"

Johanna looked down. Her dress had acquired black smudges and her hands were black, too. With the heat of the fire and the smell of cooking, it was stuffy in the kitchen and her dizziness returned.

"I . . . didn't feel so well," Johanna managed to say before collapsing in a chair. Black spots danced in her vision.

"Oh no, certainly, I can see that. Let us take those dirty things off and get you tucked into bed."

"Where is Roald?" Johanna asked weakly. She let Koby take off her cloak.

"He was in the library the last time I saw him."

Of course, where else?

The young man said, "I'll let him know that you're back. Your father was a little bit worried, and the prince got worried, too. Your father said you should not have gone out alone, and I agree. It's not safe on the streets at night."

"Nothing about what we will be doing is going to be safe."

"Maybe not, but make it as safe as possible, mistress."

He left the kitchen.

"What is his name again?" Johanna asked.

"Sebastian. I thought you'd been introduced."

"Have I?" She didn't remember. Her head felt so woolly. She pressed her hands to her face.

"Where did you go at this time of the day, mistress?"

"I went to the barn. We had agreed to meet people whose houses had been burned and had nowhere to stay there. I talked to Loesie." The full horror of what Loesie had said came back to her.

"You didn't see Nellie?"

"No. Was I supposed to?"

"She went to see her family."

"Are they all right?"

"Alive, yes, but not all right. Their house was burned and her father was injured and he's very sick. Probably won't make it through the winter."

Poor Nellie. "But she will come back here, won't she?"

"I assume she will be back tomorrow. But come on now. Do you want some bread before going to bed? I made it fresh."

Johanna shook her head. Normally she loved the warm bread, but right now, she thought she was going to be sick again.

"You do look very pale, mistress. You're not going to catch an illness, are you?"

"I don't know. I think I caught something."

"Let's take you to bed, then. Come on, let me take your arm."

Koby helped Johanna up. Now that she was used to the stuffy air, she felt fine, if very tired. They walked through the basement hallway, up the stairs to the ground floor. The sound of male voices drifted from the library.

". . . and Rinius has written a few more works, which are extremely rare," Father was saying.

Roald said, "I have read his *Theories of The Skies* in the monastery's library. It was a poor copy, but it's the only place I have ever seen one."

"Is it really as controversial as they say?"

"It's a very interesting book. Rinius claims that . . ."

At least it sounded like Roald had found someone to talk to.

Koby led her up the stairs.

Johanna turned left, but Koby pulled her to the right. "This way, mistress. Your father said that you should have his room."

"But . . ." That was embarrassing. Her room was big enough for two.

"There is a big bed in the room, and it's safer, at the back of the house."

That was true.

So they entered the room that had been her parents' sanctuary. It felt somehow wrong, but Johanna didn't have the energy to protest.

Koby took off the disgusting dress, and brought a bowl of water for Johanna to wash with. She wet the cloth and wrung it out. When the wet cloth touched her skin,

Johanna shivered deep into her bones. Yes, she was definitely not well. Sleep in a warm bed would hopefully sort that out.

Koby also brought her nightgown and then left her with the words, "I will let the men know that you're up here and sleeping." She was at the door, about to leave the room when she hesitated and turned around. "Do you think that your being unwell means that we will have a little pair of feet running around this house soon?"

"No, I . . ." Johanna was going to say that she didn't think so, but by the Triune, it could be.

Right now that she had decided that it was probably better if the children stayed away until Alexandre was gone, the city was safe and the palace rebuilt, Roald officially crowned and the two of them officially married.

But children didn't wait for that sort of thing just because you wanted them to.

Koby smiled and shut the door.

Johanna lay in the big bed in the somewhat unfamiliar room staring at the ceiling. She put her hands over her lower stomach that felt, if anything, bloated and painful. Just like if she'd eaten something disagreeable.

No, she was probably sick. She had managed to go all the way to Florisheim and stay at the river camp without once being sick. Plenty of people had gotten sick there. She was just a bit late catching up.

But . . .

It worried her.

She worried about what Loesie had said. It had been Kylian who had struck Loesie mute, Kylian who had killed her family; Kylian, who had danced with Johanna at the ball. Who had kissed her. Whom she had witnessed performing an incomplete necromancy. Who had shared dinner with her in the Guentherite Brotherhood's monastery. Forced her to stay. Forced her to . . .

She was still unsure just exactly what had happened at that time in between finishing dinner and waking up on the floor when the others came to rescue her. She feared what had happened.

So many questions.

So many fears and uncertainties.

So much magic.

Roald came into the room later. Maybe Johanna had dozed a bit, or maybe she hadn't. Father was in the hallway with him, holding the candle.

"In there," he was saying. "I hear that she wasn't feeling well."

The door shut and footsteps came across the floor.

"You're feeling sick. I won't look at you today. I'm being very quiet so that you can sleep."

"Thank you, Roald," she said.

The bed moved when he lay down, and soon after, he started snoring.

Johanna still couldn't sleep. She worried and tossed and turned.

Johanna must have dozed briefly, because all of a sudden, she woke up. Morning light came in between the curtains and the sound of voices drifted up from the hall. It was Nellie, who must have returned from her family, and someone she didn't recognise.

Johanna thought she could hear her name being mentioned. She tiptoed from the bed. Whoa, it was cold. Koby had laid out a clean dress on the bench before the dressing table. She pulled it on. The coldness of the fabric made her shiver, so she didn't think that she was quite recovered yet. Better spend some time resting by the fire today.

In the hall she found Nellie talking to a woman she remembered vaguely as having been active in the church. As soon as the woman saw Johanna, she said, "Oh!" and she dropped into a curtsy.

Well, that was embarrassing. Johanna still felt a bit uncertain on her feet. Her hair was uncombed and her dress was warm and comfortable but not the best. She wasn't fitted out to play Queen.

"There were rumours that you had made it back with the prince. Is . . . he here as well?"

"Still asleep," Johanna said.

"We've been waiting for this opportunity. Waiting for someone to tell us that not all is lost, and that we don't need to live under this tyrant and his evil church."

"I'm afraid I don't remember your name."

"Oh, I'm sorry. I'm Greetje, Your Majesty. Greetje Porter."

Oh yes, from the family that owned the grocery store. They were a customer of Father's but Johanna had always dealt with their warehouse manager.

"Please come into the kitchen where it's warm," Koby said. "It's a most nasty cold day."

They went down the stairs into the low-ceilinged basement. The servants' rooms were on both sides, many of them empty. Nellie had quickly made her room a little home again, complete with a little vase of rose hips from the garden.

The kitchen was warm. A hearty fire burned in the

hearth and a pan of soup bubbled on the stove. The air smelled of baking bread.

The smell still made Johanna feel a bit queasy although she couldn't work out if that was because she felt sick or was hungry.

They sat down around the table—sturdy and made of rough wood—and Koby poured tea.

"It's like this, Your Majesty," Greetje began. She self-consciously tucked a strand of hair in her bonnet. "When those monsters took over our city, they cowardly went for the weakest and easiest targets: people from the church. They burnt the buildings, sometimes with the Shepherds still inside. Old Shepherd Darius from the church in East End they tied to the altar and then they set fire to the building." She shuddered and stared at her tea. "As if that wasn't enough, they came after the rest of us, everyone who had involvement with the church. I don't know how they knew who these people were, other than that people like Octavio Nieland or the other nobles told them. They'd always spoken up against the church. So a lot of us hid in the cellars and the warehouses. We took things from houses where we knew that all the inhabitants were dead and they would no longer need their possessions. We didn't like doing it, but we begged the Holy Spirit for forgiveness. We had to be careful because the guards and their bears were also looting people's possessions. They were putting gold and other precious things on barges that were taken up the river. Taking all the wealth from the citizens—"

"What about the palace? I noticed they were rebuilding it."

"The tyrant wants to restore the palace, so he's left it as is, except for the main hall which he has already started repairing. But I've heard that he's finding it hard to get people to do the work."

"That's because most workers were commoners and are supporters of the Church of the Triune."

"They *were* supporters of the Church of the Triune." Her expression was grave.

An unspoken horror went between them: these people were dead.

"How many died?"

"We don't know. Hundreds, at least. It was a good thing that, when the fires broke out, not many people had gone to bed yet. When it became clear that they were after church people, we hid in cellars and warehouses. But still many were found and killed by Alexandre's men in the days after the fires."

"Are any church people still left?"

"There are. We have services in different places every couple of days. Not on a regular day, because that would make them suspicious, and we meet somewhere else every time. We have a new Shepherd. Shepherd Victor. You might know him." She smiled. "We would be most honoured if you could visit us and take prayer with us."

"Yes, I would."

"What about the most important patron of the church?"

It took Johanna a few seconds to figure out that she was talking about Roald, because he didn't strike her as being very supportive of the church. In fact, she didn't think she had ever heard him talk about the church. Strange that he should be "the most important patron". "Maybe he can come. If it's safe."

"Both of you would be most welcome. We've been looking for a sign of hope. I do believe this is it." She took

Johanna's hands. Her hands were still cold from outside. "There is a service on tomorrow night. I will send one of the boys along to pick you up."

When Greetje was gone, Koby started making breakfast and Roald came blundering down the stairs.

"Where is breakfast in this house?"

"You're in the right place. Just wait until I make some new tea. And I do believe that the bread is done." Koby gave him a thick slice of bread just out of the oven that still steamed and absorbed the butter like a sponge.

He started eating, dripping butter and jam down his chin.

He hadn't shaved for a number of days, but Johanna decided that the reddish beard made him look more serious. He looked tired, they all were.

Koby put a slice of bread in front of her. Johanna didn't feel like eating, but she picked at it a bit, because Koby was shooting her you-must-eat daggers. The jam made it better, though. Much better.

Meanwhile, Roald asked Koby questions about making bread, and as it turned out, he had some experience. "If we did something the abbot didn't like, he would make us work in the laundry or the kitchens. I didn't like the laundry, but the kitchens were all right."

"Your Majesty, that's scandalous. Did you do that many naughty things?"

"Once I said that I thought their statue of the Triune in the chapel was wrong. Once I told a brother to stop hitting a horse. Once I told the brother that his wine was off and he made it wrong, once . . ." He counted on his fingers.

Koby laughed. "You were quite the rascal, then."

"They were unfair. The work I did was fair. The horse

didn't ask to be hit, and a horse doesn't know why you hit it. The bad wine was his own fault."

Johanna reminded herself to never do anything stupid in Roald's presence, because he would remember and recount it until the end of his days.

Koby completely relaxed in his presence, and showed him her baking tray and other utensils with flour-covered hands.

Nellie announced that she had work to do, and Johanna remained at the table, clutching her cup and gradually finishing her bread.

It worried her that Greetje had so easily found out that she and Roald were back. It meant that Alexandre would find out soon enough, too. It meant that they would have to move quickly. Visit that church service and the people who gathered there. Have some sort of ceremony to make Roald's assumption of the throne official.

That gesture would be infinitely improved if she could get the crown and staff from their hiding places. Unless Alexandre had combed the palace, she was the only person who knew where they were.

But she was tired, so incredibly cold and tired.

CHAPTER 11

TRUE TO GREETJE'S word, a boy came to the house the next morning with the message that tonight's service would be held in a boatshed in East Harbour.

Johanna didn't see him. She was resting upstairs, as she had done for much of the previous day, and only came downstairs when he returned to accompany them to the secret location of the church service.

She had eaten a bit, but still felt really tired and not quite steady on her feet.

Roald and Father were in the hall. They had spent most of the day in the library. Father looked bright, if thin and a lot greyer than he had been when she left, and he was talking in a lively manner.

He had given Roald the heavy cloak that he used when going out on the boats.

When Johanna frowned at it, he said, "I have no more boats to use it on, and I'm getting too old for that sort of thing anyway. I'm getting out of the way. It's time for the young generation to take over."

He looked lonely and sad. He had always been such a proud man, at the top of his business when all this happened, and now he was reduced to having to give away his business to a rival family in order to be able to continue it. Once Johanna had dreamt of running the Brouwer Company, but even if Father could get a new ship soon and the *Lady Sara* could resume the river trade—and to be honest, what towns were left that were in a position to resume buying luxury items?—she would be too busy helping Roald.

She hugged him.

Johanna and Roald followed Nellie and the boy out into the night. His name was Pieter, he said proudly, and he was thirteen years old. He delivered messages for the church because, "I'm so small, and the guards think that I'm a kid so they never stop me." His voice sounded very young.

Clouds hung low over the city, and an occasional squall would whip cold drops of rain into Johanna's face.

Pieter carried a storm lamp and led them through alleys and back streets so that they avoided most of the spots where the guards often patrolled. He knew exactly where they went and what routes they took. Once they saw two men with a storm light, but otherwise, the night belonged to the wind and rain.

East Harbour was an area where large warehouses lined the waterfront. Most of those were fairly new and purpose-built, so that they could handle the larger vessels. This was where the large ocean ships docked and where much of the imported wares were stored before they were either sold in town or carried upriver by riverboats such as the *Lady Sara*.

It was not a place for river ships or sea cows, because

that trade was much older and took place in the main harbour.

It was extremely dark and deserted in this part of town since few people lived here, even before the fires. The seafaring ships bobbed on their moorings. The water was rough, even in this sheltered area, and waves slapped against hulls and seawalls.

The boatshed was at the end of the quay where the pier jutted into the murky waters. A faint glow in the dark indicated the presence of the lighthouse, although the structure itself blended into the darkness.

They walked along the back of the shed in single file, hair and clothing flapping in the wind. Then Pieter stopped and knocked four times at a wooden warehouse door. He said in a clear voice, "The Triune is our Saviour."

The door opened a crack, revealing the faint glow of a storm light against the rough bricks of the warehouse wall.

"I've brought them," Pieter said.

A man said, "Quick, come in. It's awful out there."

The door of the shed opened further and Nellie led Johanna and Roald inside.

To Johanna's great surprise, the ground floor of the warehouse was packed. In the low light of a few storm lamps hanging on wall hooks or hoists that were normally used to haul goods to the upper floors of the warehouse, it was hard to see who all these people were. The cranes and wooden beams cast odd shadows over the crowd, but there had to be at least a hundred people gathered here. They shuffled aside to make a path for the newcomers to the back wall of the warehouse.

Here, a storm lantern stood on a table. Someone had found a smudged, formerly white tablecloth on which stood a candle in a half-burnt candle holder that Johanna recognised as having stood on the altar in the big church.

The candle was tallow wax and smoked more than it burned. Its rancid smell spread through the shed despite the draughty air. Behind the candle against the wall leaned a framed painting that depicted the Triune: a man with a twisted body that had three heads: an old man with a beard, a salivating dog and a wraith-like figure.

Johanna folded her hands and bowed her head in a moment of reflection. Next to her, Roald stood as frozen, staring at all those people who were whispering about him. He had stuffed his hands deep in his pockets. He looked awkward and nervous.

Johanna touched him on the shoulder, but he didn't react.

People started pointing and murmuring. She could almost hear the voices. *Is that him? He doesn't look as crazy as they said he was.*

The light from the storm lamps lit the crowd from behind, gilding hats, bonnets and scarves and the puffs of mist from their breathing. Some people had no winter clothing, and they came dressed in improvised capes made from horse blankets. Some people hid their faces in hoods and shawls. Some were injured. She spotted a couple of people with bandaged hands and one man at the front had weeping injuries on one side of his face. It looked red and swollen and painful. But his face was set in a determined expression.

Nellie's mother was there, and she recognised some people from shops and the markets.

Greetje came out from between the people. "Oh, I'm so happy that you're here."

She hugged Johanna and curtsied to Roald.

Then she faced the crowd and said, "I present to you, His Excellency Crown Prince Roald of Saarland and his Consort, Johanna Brouwer."

A few people cheered. Others clapped, but most watched in silence. Whether that was because they had to stay hidden or because they didn't know what to think of Roald, Johanna didn't know.

Greetje went on to tell the people about Johanna and Roald's escape to Florisheim. Again, most remained silent. Johanna had forgotten the sort of rumours that circulated amongst the townsfolk about Roald. Probably the "idiot" view was quite strong, and they would see by the way he fidgeted that Roald wasn't, and would never be, a "normal" king who gave speeches and held balls. Seeing him potter about the rose garden was about as normal as he would ever get.

This was the part where Johanna would have to stand up and take control, but the very thought made her feel sick. Seeing all these tired faces of people who had lived through hell, she wouldn't be surprised if they refused to listen to her.

But when Greetje asked, she told their story, leaving out everything about Loesie.

" 'Tis an evil world indeed," a man declared when she finished.

Others murmured agreement. Some wanted to know if they'd had church services while they were in Florisheim, and Johanna told them about Shepherd Carolus and that some of the nobles in the group, especially the women, supported the church. That made her remember Julianna Nieland and the young men who had presumably made their way back to the *Prosperity* but needed places to stay.

"We have in our group some people who have come

back and found all their possessions burned and relatives killed. Some of these people need places to stay. I'm sure that they will work for their keep."

A man wanted to know, "Do you have someone who can write neatly without mistakes?"

"Julianna Nieland."

Some gasps went up in the audience.

A woman said, "Certainly we can't have the traitor's sister in our midst? She wouldn't go against her own brother?"

"She saw what her brother did to the people of Saardam and she fled because of his actions. She could go back to his house if she wanted, but instead she has chosen to keep away from him. She sees the evil in him. She is brave but has no place to sleep."

"But then she can sleep in our house," said a clear, young male voice. Someone had just entered and was making his way through the crowd. People stepped aside for him, and bowed.

Johanna assumed this was the Shepherd Victor.

A figure in a long hooded cloak dissolved from the crowd and came to the table-turned-altar. The garment was dark on colour, brown or black, and he held it tied with a simple rope. His face was invisible in the shadow of the hood, but he reached up and pushed the hood down.

"It is a great pleasure to welcome Your Majesty in the house of the Triune—" He froze. "Mistress Johanna!"

"Master Willems!"

Johanna stared at the young man. She'd known that Shepherd Victor was not his real name, but she had expected him to be some senior member of the church.

He came to her, his eyes shining. He took her hand and dropped to one knee. "Oh, I am so glad to see you safe and well, and about to become the queen, too. I listened to rumours and prayed and dreamed, and hoped that someone would bring news of your survival."

He had listened to the wind, she was sure, but he still continued the Church line that magic didn't exist.

"I presume you have met my wife, Greetje?"

"I met her, but I didn't know that she was your wife."

"We married after the fire. We are trying to continue life as normal as we can, to have marriages, to baptise children and hold funerals. We've had far too many of those lately. We can use some good news."

"Your parents?"

His face fell. "Died in the fire."

"Oh, I'm so sorry."

"Everyone of us has a story of loss and pain to tell. We've been trying to keep people's hopes up by holding weddings. Maybe now that you have returned, we should have a very short ceremony that we all confirm our love for each other, and that we will help each other. Let us start with the service."

People fell quiet. Johanna took Roald's hand and drew him into the audience where the people at the front made room for them.

The ceremony was simple and short. Master Willems spoke about hope and new life, new relationships. He likened the group, this little seed of resistance, to a blade of grass pushing through the snow after winter.

People prayed. Happy tears rolled over many cheeks.

At the end, the Shepherd asked Johanna and Roald to come forwards and to state officially that they were husband and wife, and that the marriage service had been conducted before a member of the church. Johanna said that it had, and that, when the hard times were over, there would be an official celebration.

"Certainly that will be a celebration of the firstborn prince or princess," a woman said.

Others agreed.

"If you were married a few months ago, we should certainly have an heir by summer," a woman said.

Johanna smiled politely but felt miserable inside.

More people gathered around and Johanna asked about people she knew, like the families of the ship's boys.

In turn, people wanted to know about survivors who had been to Florisheim with Johanna. Most of the names she mentioned met with snorts and scoffs. Of Fleuris LaFontaine someone said that it was better that he stayed there. "Never good for anything except bossing people around and complaining that the work wasn't done good enough. He would go and explain how it was done. He's never done anything himself."

The only person who met with any kind of approval was Master Deim.

"He's a decent sort," a man said. "But I thought he was from Florisheim or has family there."

"He does, but his sister-in-law is a Saarlander." Johanna remembered the picture above the hearth and the woman's awkward pledge of loyalty.

Then the meeting was over and people started filing out of the shed in small groups so as not to draw attention. In the end just Master Willems, Greetje, Nellie, Roald and Johanna were left in the coldness of the empty warehouse.

Johanna held Roald's arm and faced Master Willems, who held Greetje's arm. She was shivering in the cold.

"We are always in the last group to leave," Master

Willems said. "We turn off the lights and make the room look like the meeting never happened."

Nellie had already started sweeping dust over the floor.

"It's very good to see that you have survived," Johanna said. "But I don't understand. Father says that you've gone missing."

"He knows where I am, but that I've gone missing is the story we tell everyone. After the burning of the city, it soon became clear that Alexandre and his louts were after members of the church. That's how they got my family."

And that might be why the LaFontaine nephew had mocked about Master Willems having gone missing. He knew that Father had something to hide, because if Master Willems had really gone missing, Father would have appointed a different accountant long ago.

"I'm so sorry about your family."

He pressed his lips together. "I'm learning to move forward."

"You knew that the trouble was coming for us, didn't you? You had seen it on the wind."

"They were omens."

"Would you deny your gift, even now?"

His expression closed. "I do not speak of that thing. The Triune teaches that it is not a good thing." Even now, he could not say the word *magic*.

"I understand, but I don't think it's wise. Are we going to face Alexandre wielding prayer books while he mows us down with magic fire?"

He gave her a sharp look.

"He will come for us, and he will kill us all if we give him a chance."

"We will stay out of his way until we are so numerous that he can't fight all of us at once. He thinks we are weak and scared. The numbers of Estlanders he employs has already gone down a lot. By the time we are strong, he will have too few trusted men to fight us."

"He's recruiting people in the city."

"Only those who are easily swayed by power will come to him. The rest will not betray their family and friends."

Johanna wasn't so sure about that. If people were desperate enough, they would do anything.

Then they discussed what should be done next.

Master Willems said, "In a time like this, we cannot do much without a strong leader. The prince must assume the throne. We must hold a coronation ceremony and we must make a temporary palace."

Johanna agreed and guessed that her father's house would have to fulfil that function, although Roald would probably never satisfy the description *strong leader*. "We may be able to hold a proper coronation ceremony."

"The crown and staff were lost when the king and queen were killed," Master Willems said, gravely.

"I know. I saw the bodies in the palace. I picked up the crown and the staff and hid them."

He stared at her, open-mouthed. "You know where they are?"

"In the same place I left them, unless you've seen Alexandre wear those things."

"No, we haven't. Alexandre declares himself the regent but he never wears the crown and never carries the staff. We thought that meant the crown must have been lost."

"Mind you, they might still have been lost, but it looks like most of the palace still stands. There is a good chance that the crown and staff are still where I hid them. Alexandre hasn't done much to fix the palace up?"

He shook his head. "Most of the roof has fallen in. He can't find people to fix it."

Greetje started laughing at this, and Johanna guessed that this was one of the ways that the citizens protested against the tyrant.

"We could retrieve them and have the proper ceremony."

Master Willems' eyes shone. "That would be a slap in his face."

"We could get in through the rose garden. There is a hedge in the rose garden that surrounds a wall that's not very high and shouldn't be too hard to climb."

CHAPTER 12

MOST OF THE next day, Johanna sat in the kitchen because an icy wind had come up and there was not enough wood to heat the entire house. Father stayed in the library where, thanks to the high ceiling, it was much colder despite the fire. He said, "You young people should talk amongst yourselves."

Johanna told him not to be silly and join them, but he said that he expected a visit from Auguste LaFontaine and that the LaFontaines should not find out about his houseguests.

Which was true.

But the LaFontaine cousin stayed away, probably because of the weather. Father took his tea in the library. Roald had moved a chair from the cold formal sitting room into the kitchen, where it had stood in the corner for many years. It was a strange thing, made from some kind of twig, much thinner and smoother than willow twigs. She used to love it when she was little, because the wood would show her a large river flowing between steep rocks covered in green. It was a landscape she had never seen before or since.

She didn't know how Father had obtained the chair, but since it weighed a lot less than the traditional furniture, it had been easy for Roald to carry downstairs. He sat there now, reading a book with his feet on a footstool and the glow from the fire gilding his trousers and slippers.

The rain had turned to snow at midmorning, but the darkness was never dispelled from the house.

At some time in the afternoon came the sound of footsteps from the back yard, the kitchen door opened and Greetje came in.

"Cold out there," she said while unwrapping the shawl from her head and shaking out the snowflakes. She stood by the fire, warming her hands. Roald was deeply engrossed in a book and never looked up.

"The boys like the idea of getting the crown and staff," Greetje said, rubbing her hands. "Bert says that there is a new moon in two weeks and it might be good to break into the palace then."

"That sounds like a good idea. Could you find a couple of volunteers to come with me?"

"By the Triune, you're not planning to go yourself?"

"Who else knows where the crown and staff are?"

"You can give directions."

"I don't remember exact details. I can tell on sight once I see the room, but I don't know the palace well enough to give the men precise directions."

Greetje gave her a horrified look. "But you're the consort. You can't possibly—"

"I'm also the only person who knows where I put the crown."

She still didn't look convinced. "By the Triune, the boys

are not going to like this. My husband told me to not let you go out more than necessary. He said we will come and guide you. It's tricky enough simply walking the streets. The guards walk certain patterns. If they see you, they will sometimes stop you for a stupid reason and ask you questions to make you angry. They're trying to find an excuse to make you dependent on Alexandre. If you protest too much, he sets your house on fire. He's an evil man, possessed by the Lord of Fire. He just flicks his hand at a house and it burns."

And none of these people with powerful magic wanted to help her. Instead she was left to fight magic with virtually no magic of her own. With a church that denied the existence of magic. They didn't need more people; they needed more useful people.

"Do you want some tea?" Koby asked.

"Well, I . . ." Greetje hesitated. "Oh, why not."

It was warm in the kitchen. Koby had a pan of hot water on the stove for the washing, and after Greetje accepted the tea she took off her coat.

Underneath, she wore a dark dress of thick fabric that looked like it had once made up curtains in a house of a well-off family.

She laughed when she noticed Johanna staring at it. "The dress is a bit odd, I admit, but I had to make something that would accommodate my condition." She joined her hands and pushed down the fabric under her belly. It showed a clear swelling.

Johanna stared. "These are poor times to be having a child."

"The times are as good or bad as you make them. Times may be hard, but there is nothing I can change about them. These hard times are when I got married, and

I'm not letting that stand in the way of having a family." She sipped from her tea.

Koby picked up the pan and carried it, steaming and all, into the laundry, leaving Johanna and Greetje at the table. Roald was still reading. Had he even noticed that they had a visitor and were talking about retrieving the symbols of his family?

Johanna played with her cup, looking at Greetje from the corner of her eye. "How do you know . . . that you're going to be having a child? Like, in the very beginning?"

"Well, you don't bleed, of course. You start to feel strange sometimes. Puffy, or full, or sick sometimes, and you can faint, but that hasn't happened to me. And then you notice that nothing fits anymore so you have to get special dresses."

"Do you feel the child move inside you?"

"Yes, but that's not until later. Why are you asking? Are you. . . ?"

"I don't know." And she truly didn't. With all the things that had been going on, Johanna couldn't remember when she had last bled. She remembered the last time she'd been disappointed about it, but she thought there had been another time. In which case it was probably much too early to tell, and in which case . . . no, she wasn't going to think about what happened in the Guentherite farmhouse with Kylian. She pushed down her unease. She asked, "How long did you notice this after you were married?"

"It didn't take me long at all. We were married and that night he took me to bed and I never bled since."

Johanna gritted her teeth. For some people, it was so easy. "It took Queen Cygna a number of years."

"That's true. Maybe it's a royal family thing."

Maybe, too, people who weren't entirely normal couldn't have children. She'd heard of some people called simple or idiots, but none she knew of had ever had children.

She shuddered.

Which was worse: that she never had a child, that the child was afflicted with the same condition as Roald, or, heaven forbid, that Kylian had bewitched her, had his way with her and the child was his?

Blood rose to her cheeks.

All of a sudden, it was too hot and stuffy in the kitchen. She rose so quickly that her chair almost fell over. She ran out of the kitchen, through the laundry, past Koby who was scrubbing clothes in the big wash tub, and out the back door.

"Mistress Johanna!" Koby protested.

Johanna stopped, panting in the back courtyard where the neat garden was brown for winter. A drift of fat snowflakes fell from the sky.

She hugged herself against the cold. The snow melted where it hit her arms. Her stomach was churning. Shooting pains went through her breasts. They felt as hard as rocks. Those were all signs, weren't they?

Koby came out into the snow. "Mistress? What are you doing out here?"

"I just . . . couldn't breathe in there."

"It's cold and wet out here. Come inside." She put an arm on Johanna's shoulder, guiding her back into the kitchen.

Greetje raised her eyebrows.

"I'm not very well," Johanna said.

Greetje and Koby exchanged a knowing look.

Koby said, "Not to be jumping to conclusions too

quickly, mistress, but I think there is a good chance that we'll have the patter of little feet in summer."

Roald looked up with a huh–what? expression.

"And there we have the father to be."

Roald frowned at her. He looked genuinely puzzled, as if he didn't think that all those nights that she had sat astride him would have any consequences. There had been so many of those nights.

Of course any child she had was his. Any other possibility was simply put into her head by magic. They wanted her to feel uncertain.

She was not going to let her mind wander down silly winding tracks. If there was going to be a prince or princess, he or she was of Carmine blood.

A few days later Johanna went to another Church service, this time at someone's house at the very edge of the city. Greetje had drummed up more volunteers for her trip to the palace than she needed. She'd hoped to get two or three men, but she ended up with eight.

Some of the men were adamant that she should not go. "You're the Queen. If we lose you, our efforts at resisting Alexandre will have been for nothing."

"I know where these things are. I know the palace better than any of you. I can't let you go inside without a guide. You might get lost."

The men were all warehouse workers and shipbuilders and carpenters. None of them had ever set foot inside the palace, so they reluctantly had to agree to let her come.

They worked out a plan. They would do it on the night of the next new moon. A couple of men would hide a ladder in the reeds along the river on the outside the palace garden. They would climb in through the Queen's rose garden and then through the garden room and the big ballroom, into the royal family's living quarters.

"That is, if the palace hasn't been looted," Greetje said.

Johanna hoped not, and the signs were good. The only one who would have looted the palace would be Alexandre.

She did wonder why he didn't live in the palace, especially because, since there was such a shortage of housing, it seemed silly to leave such a large building vacant.

The day after, Auguste LaFontaine came back to the house. Johanna didn't see him come in, but Koby told her that he was upstairs when Johanna came back from the markets. She had been trying to buy some fabric because a couple more days of feeling weird and sometimes near fainting convinced her that Koby was probably right, and she intended to ask Nellie to make a dress for her. Except she had come back empty-handed, because everyone had bought all available fabric for the winter.

Voices drifted through the house from the hall when she came into the kitchen. The conversation didn't sound friendly. Koby put her finger to her lips.

Johanna quietly sneaked up the stairs to the point where the steps switched back in the other direction and she would be in view of the people in the hall.

An arrogant-sounding voice said, "I've given you enough time to think about it. I don't want to talk or negotiate about it again. You either sign that agreement and lead a happy life or you don't and we'll take your business from you when you're dead."

Father said, "You'll get it anyway. This document is an instrument of blackmail."

"You dare to be rude to me? You, an old man with no friends and no children?"

Johanna cringed. *Father, we don't have time for this.*

"I've thought about your proposition, and I do not want to accept it. I understood that this choice was up to me."

"Do you really choose to let your business die through a lack of ships?"

"I'll replace the ship. I'll carry on. If, when the time comes, I have not located any of my or my former wife's family, I will pick a loyal employee and give the company to him."

The man made sputtering noises. "Yes, well, don't ask for our help ever again."

"I never asked for help in the first place. I listened to your proposal because I thought it might work, but I've decided that it won't."

"Well then," Auguste scoffed. "Well . . . good luck. Because you'll need it."

There were footsteps in the hall. The door opened and slammed shut.

Johanna ran up the stairs. Father stood in the hallway, bolting the front door. He turned around and smiled when his eyes met Johanna's.

"Why did you do that, Father?"

"Because I'm not going to crawl at their feet anymore. Having you here means that I don't have to do that. I was never much at ease with the idea of taking such a young woman as wife either, and it would have been a terrible thing for all concerned."

"Oh, Father." She hugged him.

She liked how he was proud and didn't give in to pressure—had he ever given in to pressure in his life?—but it would draw attention from Alexandre. He might investigate or keep a close eye on Father, because Father was supposed to be widowed, lonely and unhappy. If he was none of those things, it would arouse suspicion.

This meant that any action against Alexandre would have to come sooner rather than later.

CHAPTER 13

AT NIGHT, Johanna worried. Their group was small and disorganised, and had no magicians. Alexandre controlled the guards, of which there were fewer than before, but still more than enough to wipe their entire group off the world. The Church followers weren't ready for a conflict and it seemed that they were headed for one.

She sat in the kitchen until everyone else had gone to bed, listening to the wind whistle around the corners and gutters.

She should go to sleep, but in the past few days she had slept so much that she wasn't tired. But it was getting cold in this kitchen, so she picked up the candle and carried it upstairs. Roald lay on his stomach, his face squished in the pillow and turned to her. His breathing was soft and regular.

She pulled her dress over her head and lifted her underdress to look at her pale body in the mirror. The skin over her breasts was tight and the tissue underneath felt like a bag filled with beans. It was sore at the slightest touch of her fingertips. They seemed larger. Definitely more filled. She slid her hand over her stomach and then puffed it out to make it seem more round.

By the Triune, it was an unfortunate thing to happen right now. And scary, too. Maybe Greetje was all upbeat about it, but Mother had died while carrying a brother or sister for her. Father had told her that when it became clear that Mother was expecting Johanna, she had signed her will, mainly to, in the event of her death, keep the Aroden family from claiming a part of the Brouwer Company.

Johanna should go and see a lawyer.

Maybe.

Maybe in a day or two, it would all prove to be a false alarm and she would have worried for nothing. Or hoped for nothing, she didn't know which.

They had a revolution to fight and a tyrant to drive from the city. There was no time for sickness and babies.

She let the nightdress fall and climbed into bed. Then she blew out the candle.

In the darkness, Roald said, "You were looking at yourself."

She hadn't realised he was awake.

He slid a hand over her side and up to her breast.

"Ow."

He withdrew. "That hurts?"

"Yes. It's nothing to do with you. It's just . . . sore." She thought for a while, and then decided what the heck. "Roald, I think I'm having a child."

He took quite a while to process that. She expected questions about how that worked, but then she remembered that he had read books about human anatomy and probably knew better than anyone how that worked.

"Like the cows," he said in a matter-of-fact way.

"I suppose." She was a bit miffed to be compared with a cow, but if that made him happy . . .

"I used to have to get up at night and check on the cows when they were calving. Sometimes there was one where the calf was stuck, and I'd have to put my hand in and push it right. It was messy. The calf used to come out covered in a blue-white sac, with blood and water. Like that?"

"Well . . ." *Thanks, Roald, for the detail I didn't need to know.* "I suppose so." By the Triune, now she felt ill again.

"That's all right." He sounded very confident. "I can help." He slid his hand down her side and between her legs. "It comes out here."

"Thank you, Roald, but—oh!" That whole area was sensitive, in a good way.

"Does that hurt, too?"

"No. It feels . . . good."

"Do you want me to look at you?"

"Well, I . . ." She wasn't sure. Didn't they always say to be really careful in the beginning? But then, didn't she want this to be a false alarm? Maybe she was just panicking and felt this way because her bleeding was really late. Maybe it would get the bleeding started. She lifted her leg over him.

Normally, she would be a bit sore when he went inside her, but this time, the waves of pleasure hit her almost straight away, and twice more immediately afterwards. When he finished and she lay in the warm hollow against his body, the entire bottom half of her body was throbbing and glowing. There was no doubt left in her mind that she was with child.

This became even more clear the next morning when

she ate two healthy slices of Koby's bread and then had to run outside to empty her stomach. No one saw her do that—it was a terrible thing because people went hungry in town, and the bread was very good.

It had snowed overnight and Johanna used her wooden shoe to push snow over the patch so that hopefully no one would notice. But when she was inside, of course, she felt hungry again. She didn't dare eat, but that made her feel even sicker and she vomited again, in the washbowl upstairs, because there wasn't anywhere else to do it. She stood there, awkwardly holding the porcelain washbowl with a smelly puddle of brown in the bottom, wondering how to discreetly get rid of it, when Nellie came in.

"Oh, oh, Mistress Johanna. Give that to me and go to bed. You need lots of rest in your condition."

Johanna protested weakly that she was hungry but Nellie wouldn't have a bar of it, and so she lay in bed again, sick and hungry, her whole body throbbing.

This was the bed where her mother had lain in the same condition, the bed where Johanna had been born and where, two years later, her mother had died while carrying a brother or sister. Unless something dramatic happened and they could defeat Alexandre, Johanna might do most of those same things here.

Johanna tried some water, but that came back out straight away, so she got dressed and went downstairs and convinced Koby that she needed something to eat that wasn't bread because her stomach didn't like it. Koby gave her some cheese and that made her feel much better.

So much better, in fact, that she went back to worrying about how to deal with the fact that the band of Church followers would soon face Alexandre and they were nowhere near ready.

Failing a magician, they needed all the people they could recruit to the cause, and something needed to be done about this soon.

In the afternoon, when Nellie would let her leave the house, she went to see the cheese seller Leo at the markets, but found the market place infested with guards. They walked between the stalls looking at produce, looking at people, talking to people. They were mostly traitors: Saarlander men in the employ of the occupying force. They wore blue uniforms, some with shiny buttons, but most of the jackets looked a little the worse for wear. Johanna wondered where they had come from and who had worn them previously.

A couple stood around a man who was said to have stolen an apple. He was crying about not having enough to eat and having lost everything and the guards threatened to take off his shirt and beat him.

Really, they would do that?

In Saardam, they'd risen above such barbaric processes long ago. That just went to show that *the veneer of civilisation is thin*, one of the things Master Deim loved to say.

Johanna very much wanted to tell those arrogant young men in their new suits that this wasn't how Saarlanders treated each other, but had to keep walking because she couldn't afford to get involved. They might recognise her. They would report her to Alexandre or Octavio Nieland.

Leo was at the usual table with his cheeses. Not as many as before the fires, Johanna noticed. He raised his eyebrows at Johanna and made all sorts of hand gestures that probably meant that she had better not talk about anything that she didn't want anyone else to hear. So she told him that she was interested in buying a horse.

His face cleared up. "Oh, you must have heard about the horse that I bought from a group of travellers."

"I was going to put a bid on that horse," said the farmer in the next stall.

"No, I," said the stallholder across the aisle.

About ten people said they were interested in the horse, and Leo was trying to tell everyone where they could view this horse, when a guard turned up.

He stopped at Leo's stall and asked him a question that Johanna couldn't hear. Leo replied something about having found the horse wandering around.

"If it's found to be an escaped coach horse, you will be charged with theft."

"I didn't steal anything. I bought it, fair and square."

"The horse trade is not your normal business."

"Then am I not allowed to earn some extra money and help a fellow out?"

Johanna rounded to corner of the aisle and stopped, heart thudding. The voices of Leo and the guard drifted on the wind, but she couldn't figure out what they said.

"That particular low-life of a man does that all the time," a merchant wife said to Johanna, while jerking her head in the direction of the guard. "Joined this tyrant as soon as he started calling for local volunteers. He was always a funny character, but I never thought he'd betray us."

"I always said he would," added another stallholder. "He's a weaselly little man who likes to pretend he's more than he is, grovelling for this tyrant and Octavio Nieland."

Johanna managed to get them to tell her where Leo's warehouse was and then she continued on her way.

CHAPTER 14

BEFORE JOHANNA had left the markets, there was a to-do at the mayor's house. While she had talked to Leo, more people had gathered in front of the house, kept away from the steps that led up to the front door by a handful of guards.

The door to the house and a third guard came out, holding a trumpet with blue tassels. Some people cheered, others called out, holding out their hands like beggars.

The man stopped right in front of the railing at the top of the steps and faced the crowd. He put the trumpet to his mouth and played a fanfare, loud and clear. The sound echoed over the square

The door opened again and a man dressed in blue appeared on the top of the steps. Blue cape, blue trousers, blue jacket and a white shirt with excessive ruffles. He was thin and wore his honey-coloured hair in a ponytail that stuck out from under his wide-brimmed hat. His boots were of the thick-soled type that made the wearer appear taller, black and polished with shiny buckles.

While he stood at the top of the stairs surveying the

crowd, another two men came out of the door, each carrying one end of a box that looked like a travel chest. They manoeuvred this thing down the stairs and set it on the ground before the line of people.

The man in blue, whom Johanna had never seen but assumed was Alexandre Trebuchet, came down the stairs in an effortless glide.

The people in the queue called out to him.

"Please, lord, help an old woman."

"Please, lord, my children are sick and we have no house."

"Please, we need wood for the fire."

Alexandre simply walked past them without looking, his chin in the air, ignoring all their calls. A couple of men followed him, all dressed in finery. One of those men was Octavio Nieland. He and another man went to the box and stood next to it, crossing their arms over their chests. A lot of people in that line were looking at the box with wide eyes.

Johanna pulled the hood of the cloak further over her face and retreated further into the nearby stall. It sold eggs and pears, dried beans and flour. She hoped no one would recognise her.

Alexandre and his men walked along the perimeter of the markets past the boarded up weigh house and the makeshift replacement, past the ruins of the house on the corner, to the empty block where the church had stood.

One of the men produced a roll of paper, which he unrolled and held up for Alexandre to see.

"It be bad news, what that man is doing," said the stall-holder, a short woman whose well-fed appearance showed no signs of hardship.

"I assume he's rebuilding the church?"

"That, he is," a man said, presumably her husband. "I've not seen the plans myself, but I hear from my cousin who is a carpenter that it's quite a monstrous thing he's building. That other man over there is Charles DeLuc from Burovia." Johanna presumed that he meant the dark-haired man who was pointing at the plans. "He's known for designing ridiculously expensive buildings."

The farmer in the next stall laughed. "That thing will take so much stone, the ground is too soft for it. It will sink sideways before they ever get to put the roof on it."

A few others agreed with this and went on to debate whether the new church would be more elaborate than the old church; and since that church had been made of wood, it had to be.

Johanna asked, "Do any of you know what that thing is they're building in the harbour?"

"No, lady, not a clue, but they're working hard at it. There's a full team of men turning up there every morning. They get every single brick the brickmakers can produce that we haven't already managed to get. He's using his own men to build it and they don't come into town and don't talk to anyone else."

"I think it's some kind of oven for making bricks," another man said.

"I think it's for building ships," said the farmer. "Why else would they build it in that place?"

Johanna was reminded of the strange activities going on at the Guentherite Brotherhood's farm. The hole in the ground and the black rock that was taken out. And the stranger activities at the Abbott's summer residence.

She asked, "Have you seen any ships bringing in iron?"

There were headshakes at this. "Why iron?"

"We saw similar strange things being built all along the

river. Mostly there are monks of the Guentherite order involved. They dig holes in the ground, take out black rock and make iron. No one knows why."

The stallholder's wife said, "There were some monks here in autumn, but they left a few weeks ago. We thought it was to do with their church. People were saying that the Belaman Church got angry with the Church of the Triune and the Holy Father said that the Church of the Triune broke church teachings and banished them."

"Yeah, I heard that, too," said the man in the next stall.

That part of the rumours was true. The Belaman Church encouraged magic. Were they going to take their ghosts, black rock and iron into Saardam? Were they performing necromancy?

She shivered.

All the construction works along the river were part of a plan. She wondered what had gone wrong at the Abbot's summer residence and how much that had delayed their construction. Something evil was being created and should be stopped. Alexandre should *not* build a church here, in the place where she used to come most days for the Shepherd Romulus' service. Where the wooden pews told her their stories, and where on most mornings, the Shepherd could be seen teaching children and giving poor families food and clothing.

Alexandre and his party had walked around the bare and muddy building site and come back to the house, where Octavio and the other man still stood on either side of the chest.

The people in the queue again started yelling their pleas at him.

An old woman fell to her knees. "Please, my son is ill and I have no way to feed him. Please, lord, have mercy."

Johanna had to look away. It was embarrassing to see citizens lower themselves to this level.

Alexandre walked past the row. At the bottom of the stairs, he said something to one of his guard companions. The man went to Octavio. He said something, bowed and Octavio opened the lid. He lifted out a bag that looked like it contained potatoes.

He gave it to the guard, who put this on the ground in between the chest and the row of waiting people. As soon as he stepped back, a number of the closest people in the queue ran for it. Two men reached the bag at the same time and were pulling both ends. A woman was hitting one of the men on the head. The queue dissolved. Everyone was screaming. People gathered to watch, blocking Johanna's view. Eventually one of the men came out of the melee carrying the bag on his shoulder.

Alexandre stood at the top of the stairs, watching the spectacle. He nodded.

Octavio gave the soldier another bag, which he placed at a different spot. The process repeated, and so it went on a few times before the chest was empty and two soldiers carried it back up the stairs and inside the house.

Alexandre followed the men inside and the door shut.

Johanna felt sick. That was the worst, most revolting treatment of unfortunate people she had seen in her life, and Octavio was just doing the man's bidding. Why?

The beggars in the queue went back to their places, except the ones who had scored gifts. They gathered in a group to compare their loot.

Johanna met the eyes of a man in the queue. She had seen him before. His name was Joseph and he used to work in the Nieland warehouse. As she emerged from between the market stalls and crossed to the queue, he looked down, as if ashamed for taking part in this spectacle.

"Why do you beg him for help?" Johanna asked. "He's just doing this to make you dependent on him and make you look like a dumbwit."

"I'd rather be a dumbwit than dead, lady. Our houses were burnt and we have no food. What else are we supposed to do?"

"Maintain your pride."

"We can't eat pride. He gives us food every day, or we wouldn't stand here waiting. We're not grateful and don't bow to him. We just prefer to eat and not starve."

"So what if I said that you could get work somewhere and you'd be paid an honest wage for what you earned? And that you could use it to buy your own food?"

He laughed. "You mean a job, miss? There are no more jobs. The shops are gone and the merchants are gone. The warehouses are all empty. You don't see any of that in your rich house, lady, but that's the way it is for most of us."

Many in the queue had gathered around. Most of them wore many layers of clothes, no doubt a fair few stolen.

"Do you sit here all night?"

"Most of us have nowhere else to go."

"Many of the warehouses are abandoned. Why don't you go in there?"

"And run foul of the bears? No, thank you. We're weak, and most of us injured."

"If there are no jobs, can you make your own jobs?"

"You're dreaming, mistress. How can we make our own jobs?"

"What needs to be done most in this city?"

The looked at her, puzzled.

"We need to fix all the houses," a young woman at his back said.

"Precisely. So we fix up houses that are abandoned. We don't want another fire and we don't have much wood, so we build them from stone."

The man laughed. "Someone needs to pay for the stone."

"We make bricks from clay. There is a lot of clay around. There are brick pits. Any of you know how to make bricks?"

A few hands went up, hesitantly.

He still didn't seem to be convinced. "But what about food?"

"I know where to find food. It's not going to be wonderful, but you can survive through winter. There are many farms upriver that lie abandoned. The farmers were killed and the cows are walking free, the barns are full of hay and the orchards full of apples. None of it is good quality, but it will get you through winter. Instead of begging, you could go out there, work the farms and make the bricks. We will ship them into town."

"But winter is coming."

"Especially now that winter is coming. You don't want to rely on this man's handouts anymore. Because one day, he will ask you to do something for the food, and it's not going to be anything nice."

He gave her a dubious look. Oh, yes, she forgot that some of the townsfolk looked down on farmers. Loesie knew all about that.

The young woman's eyes were wide. "I understand what she wants. There's a lot of folk in the country who won't be needing their houses anymore. We fix up the houses and they're ours."

"They're farms, Dora."

"But they're safe and dry."

"That's exactly what I mean," Johanna said. "You don't need this foul man's handouts or his help. If you go upriver, you'll find two of our ships moored at a jetty. Tell the men who are with those ships what you're doing. They'll help you."

"Alexandre will come after us and kill us."

"If there are enough of you, let him try. I think he's got enough trouble keeping people in town in line. Also, most of his guards are Estlander mercenaries. They can be bought. Find out what their currency is."

There were some alarmed looks at this.

The man who had scored the potato bag had returned with wood and was now trying to make a fire. A few others helped him. A woman brought a pot and set about setting it up on piles of rubble and cooking. From the way others helped, she deduced that the people shared the spoils of Alexandre's donations and she didn't quite understand why the fight had been necessary.

"Who are you, lady?" the young woman Dora asked.

"I know who she is," Joseph said, but the others shushed him.

He whispered in Dora's ear. Her eyes widened, and she curtsied.

Joseph muttered, "Don't do that. Guards are watching." Then to Johanna, "You better move, mistress."

Johanna did. She was glad to see that when she walked away, a number of people picked up their blankets and left the queue.

CHAPTER 15

"LOOK," ROALD SAID when he sat down at the dinner table a few days later. He produced a sheet of paper with a drawing of some magical creature on it. The thing looked like a snake, but it had wings. He had drawn exquisite scales and featherless, leathery wings. "This is a fire dragon. It is a magical creature of the east."

Father took the drawing from him, put in his eyeglass and studied it. "You say this creature was at the site of the Guentherite Abbot's summer residence?"

"I didn't actually see it, but they did."

Johanna said, "There was only one man who said he'd seen it, and there were no other witnesses. He could have seen anything." Seriously, did they have to talk about this now? Were there no more important things to discuss?

"He said a fire dragon," Roald said. "I was there, I heard it."

"Yes, but how would he know what a fire dragon looked like if he'd never seen one before?"

Roald frowned at her. "It's in the book I read."

"What if he hasn't read the book?"

He frowned in a how-can-he-not-have-read-the-book way.

Father said, "The fire dragons are said to have been brought by the eastern traders sometimes. I've never seen any, but I've met eastern traders. I bought the chair that you've been using in the kitchen off them. There are many rumours that they want to come here and conduct trade with us. They wouldn't attack us with fire dragons if they wanted to trade."

That was true; and for all the talk there had been about eastern traders, one had yet to turn up.

"Do they have books?" Roald asked.

"I suspect they do, but we probably won't be able to read them."

Johanna heaved a sigh. She didn't have the patience for this type of discussion right now, so she changed the subject. "Well, we're going into the palace tonight to retrieve your father's crown and staff."

Father gave her a sharp look. "Are you sure you're not going to run into any patrols?"

"No, but I'm the only one who knows where they are."

"It's dangerous, Johanna."

"I know, but without the crown we have no king."

She looked at Roald, but it was pointless getting angry at him. It was not as if he would be any use if he came anyway. He would be more likely to give them away. Let him play with his dragons.

He had the book open on the table next to him, running his finger along the line as he read. "It says that fire dragons are not always dangerous."

"If any eastern traders had come up the river, we would have seen them," she said, sounding more frustrated than she should. "Whatever happened at the Guentherite Abbot's summer residence, it was a not a fire dragon. It could have been something magical, but I think it's more likely that one of their mysterious machines caught fire. If the black rock burns so well, it might have made quite a show."

"But he said it was a fire dragon," Roald protested.

"He might have been wrong. He might have heard about fire dragons and might have thought that this was one."

Arguing about it was doubly pointless. Roald did not understand the concept of lies or untruths.

"Anyway, I have to go." Johanna rose from the table and gave Father a kiss at the top of his forehead. "Don't look so worried. I'll be back."

Johanna went upstairs. Earlier in the week, she had found some of Father's old work clothes in the wardrobe in the hallway. The trousers were too big but she tied them with a rope. The jacket was also too big, and heavy, but it was warm. She wound a scarf around her neck and pulled one section over her nose and mouth and another across her forehead before putting on the cloak and pulling the hood up. The mirror showed her a figure of undetermined gender, with just the eyes showing in the shadow of the cloak.

Like this, she went downstairs where she found her boots. Father and Roald's voices drifted from the dining room. They were still talking about dragons.

Johanna went down to the basement and out through the back door. It was just as well that they had chosen the night of the new moon, because it was completely cloudless. The night was still and there would probably be frost tonight.

Johanna saw no guards, no soldiers and no sign of life except a cat that gave her a fright when it ran off from a dark spot close to her with a protesting *mrrreeeooow!*

The party of helpers waited at the boatshed in East Harbour where Johanna had first been to the service. There were nine of them, including Master Willems, who had insisted on coming. They all wore dark clothing and head coverings and in the darkness, they were all just shapes and Johanna couldn't begin to distinguish who was who. They had three storm lamps, but they met in darkness to save oil for when they were in the palace.

They decided to split up because that would draw less attention. Master Willems went with Johanna's group. Apparently, some other men had already taken the ladder to a nearby hiding place and needed to retrieve it. They also had two storm lights which they would light once they were inside the palace garden.

They left the warehouse, walking quietly through East Harbour so as not to draw the attention of the guard patrols with the bears. They saw a patrol once, but at a distance.

The palace lay on a little rise directly along the river. The gardens, including the Queen's rose garden, ran between the hillock and along the riverbank. It had its own jetty for small riverboats. A path led from the western pier of the main harbour along the bottom of the seawall. During storm tides, the water would be lapping at the stone, but normally there was a muddy beach where boys would cast out fishing lines and search for crabs and worms to use as bait. A few floating fishing sheds bobbed on their moorings. Nets hung on drying racks. The mud breathed a salty tang that came with the brackish water.

Johanna followed the men in her group along the soft and slippery ground until they came to the back of the wall that surrounded the palace garden. The rest of the group were already waiting there. They had retrieved the ladder.

A man placed it against the wall and climbed on top. He looked around and came back down again.

"The land on the other side is higher than on this side. There are some bushes, and I think we can just jump into them and won't need to use the ladder."

Johanna nodded. She already knew this. Kylian had done that on the night of the fires.

The first men climbed over.

When Johanna's turn came, they wanted to help her, but months of climbing up and down that ladder into the *Lady Sara*'s hold had made her an expert in climbing ladders. She was on the wall in no time, and lowered herself into the leafless branches of the hedge that did not look like a hedge anymore.

The rose garden was a riot of unkempt shrubs. The lawn had not been cut for months and the dead grass lay like a mat on the ground. The fountain was dry, the basin cracked, and the large statue of the Triune was gone. Deep gouges in the grass showed where it had been dragged away. Someone had vandalised the Queen's benches.

She remembered sitting here with Kylian while he remarked how ugly the statue was. Back then, she had thought he was saying these things just to get a reaction out of her, but it turned out that his plans were much more sinister than that.

The men lit the storm lanterns and ran in single file

towards the palace, where the smashed windows of the garden room reflected the glow from the storm lamps like jagged shards in the night.

At the bottom of the garden steps, the grass had been dug up. There were two longitudinal mounds of dirt, and both grew a selection of weeds and daisies.

Someone had placed a stone tile on each mound and had written something on it.

Johanna stopped.

"Come on, keep going," one of the men whispered.

"Come over here with the light," she said.

He did.

The inscription on both stones was simple and crudely scratched by someone who clearly wasn't a stonemason. The closest one said, *Queen Cygna Gunhilde Savorsen Carmine* and the other one *King Nicholaos Carmine de Lacoeur van Leeuwen.*

Johanna knelt, and next to her, Master Willems did the same.

"By the love of the Triune, we pray for salvation," he said. "We pray for our king and queen and that they have been delivered from this cruel world and look upon us with smiles. We pray that the only rightful house will return to the throne and that our actions will help."

He rose, and Johanna did the same. He took her hand. They stood for a while, looking at the graves of their king and queen.

Johanna was glad that someone had been here to bury them. In her heart she knew: this would once again be a beautiful, peaceful garden. The statue of the Triune would be found and brought back. The fountain would be fixed. The graves would have proper headstones and flowers.

There would be roses all around, and swans in the pond. Lots of swans.

"Come on," one of the men said. "We need to go. I don't want to be caught here."

After one last look, Johanna followed the others up the steps to the garden room.

CHAPTER 16

THE AIR IN the palace was cold and damp. The cloying scent of stale smoke crept through the layers of Johanna's shawl.

Thick layers of dust had accumulated on the floor in the garden room and spiders had covered walls, ceilings and furniture in their silky webs, as if the room had lain abandoned since that night. Glass from the broken windows littered the floor and crunched underfoot. Curtains were stained from being exposed to the weather and ripped to shreds from catching on the shards of glass. All the fine vases that had stood along both sides of the room had been smashed. Some of the doors into the hall had deep gouges, as if someone had taken to the wood with an axe. Johanna remembered hiding here while the people in the hall next door were ruthlessly murdered.

Shards of glass and pottery lay scattered across Celine's grave. One of the young men stopped to read the inscription in the marble slab.

"Across there," Johanna whispered, pointing at the dark entrance to the ballroom. Master Willems went first, carrying the light. But he stopped suddenly a few steps into the room and muttered, "By the Holy Ghost."

Johanna looked past him. While someone had buried the king and queen in the garden, many of the nobles in the ballroom had not been so lucky. In between the jumble of ruined tables, rotting tablecloths and shards of glass, she counted at least five skeletons, some still with scraps of silk clothing attached. Here, too, spiders had woven the dreadful scene into an ethereal tableau.

"By the Triune," one of the men said. "I didn't know there were that many spiders in the world."

Johanna drew the shawl up over her nose, even though the cold stifled whatever smell still lingered after all this time. She felt sick.

They walked across the ballroom in single file. Johanna followed Master Willems with the light, picking his way through the rubble. The thick layer of dust on the floor muffled their footsteps.

In the far corner, the roof to the main hall had caved in and starlight peeped through the gaps between the broken rafters.

They left the ballroom through the main doors into the foyer. The doors to the palace forecourt were shut, as Johanna had already seen from outside. The foyer to the main hall was the only place where there had been some attempt at cleaning up. All the rubble and mess had been swept into a heap. A wheelbarrow still stood here, half full, with a shovel on the ground next to it, as if the workmen had been called away and never returned.

This was where Johanna had stood looking out over the city, seeing the creatures made of fire. This was where panic had struck the attendants of the ball. This place was a tomb, a shrine to that terrible day.

"I don't like this place," one of the men said.

"Keep yer mouth shut and keep going," someone else said.

But Johanna agreed with the first man. There was something about this place that gave her the shivers. She kept looking over her shoulders, expecting . . . she didn't know what. Something magical. A bear, a fire demon, a ghost. So many people had died a violent death on the steps outside, in this room and the ballroom.

"This way." She had to clamp her jaws to stop her teeth chattering.

Master Willems led the party into the corridor to the right that went to the king and queen's private quarters. The storm light cast long shadows over the walls that moved and danced as they walked. This part of the palace was not as dusty and hadn't been exposed to the weather. They passed a few doors. Some of the rooms had been emptied, but all the pretty furniture still stood in the hall-way, now covered in dusty spider webs, waiting for the people who were going to take the loot, but who had never returned. Or who had, judging by a pair of shoes with cloth-covered bones attached, never left.

The air here was dry, but laced with the foulness of death. Things skittered in the dark beyond the reach of the lantern's light.

Johanna stopped at the entrance to a larger room. "This is the room where I found them."

Master Willems went to the door and held the light inside.

The room seemed untouched except for the fact that the bodies were gone. The couch still stood where it had before, as did the table, both covered in dust and spider webs. In her mind, Johanna could still see the crown where it had rolled under the table. And the staff that had been caught under the king's body. She'd had to roll him on his back to retrieve it. She remembered the mess of the gaping wound in his stomach. The carpet was dusty and smudged. Were those dark stains dried blood?

She shivered.

"In here?" Master Willems asked.

"No. This is where they were killed. I hid the crown and staff a few doors down. There is a broom cupboard." She spoke softly, but her voice sounded loud in her ears.

"Let's go then. I really don't like it here."

A bit further down the hall, Johanna found the broom cupboard, untouched. She reached up the top shelf where she couldn't see and under a pile of cleaning cloths, her hands found both crown and staff, where she had put them.

As she lifted the crown off the shelf, its weight heavy in her hands, the enormous sense of importance washed over her. It was only a piece of metal, but it symbolised the hope of all Saarlanders. The staff was a piece of wood with a gold tip in the shape of a lion's head with jewels for eyes. It was beautifully made, but she knew for sure that the jewellery made by Lurezian master smiths these days was more intricate. Yet the wood showed her images of the great hall full of nobles in their finery, bowing as the king entered. She carried the pride of the Carmine House in her hands.

She turned to the others, holding out both precious items.

"Heaven be praised," Master Willems said.

A breeze wafted through the corridor, making the flame in the lamp flap. Johanna's skin pricked.

She peered into the darkness at the far end of the corridor. "Why is it so windy?"

"There are probably some doors open," one of the men said. He sounded as uneasy as Johanna felt.

The night had been cloudless and still, not the type of weather for a breeze.

Johanna had an awful feeling that they were about to find out why Alexandre had not done anything with the palace and why he didn't live here, why people had left a wheelbarrow and a shovel and had gotten no further than a cursory tidy-up of the hall and had never collected the precious furniture.

"Quick, let's get out of here," Master Willems said. He was looking over his shoulder, his eyes wide. What had he seen on that breeze?

One of the men took off his jacket and Johanna rolled the crown and staff inside. She pulled a folded cloth from the broom cupboard, which turned out to be an old sheet, tied it around the precious loot, and tied that around her waist.

They left quickly, the same way they had come. Through the corridor, the foyer, through the hall and into the ballroom. Master Willems walked at the front, but the flapping flame from the storm lamp barely produced enough light for Johanna to see. It was as if a darkness had descended on the air that took away any light and a cold had crept into the building that settled in her bones.

Master Willems stopped abruptly at the door into the garden room.

"Someone out there," he whispered.

Johanna peered into the room, but saw nothing except broken vases and furniture covered in spider webs.

There was a small sound, a snort or grumble, made by a human or large animal.

Master Willems slid the covers over the light's windows, plunging the room into total darkness.

Johanna stood still for a while, staring into the night, waiting for her eyes to see where a human couldn't possibly see, listening, holding her breath and trying to hear over the thudding of her heart. The sound came again from somewhere in the darkness: the growl of some sort of animal, like a dog, or a bear.

"What's that?" someone whispered.

"It may be a good idea to split up," Master Willems said, not answering the question.

"What did you see in that breeze?" Johanna asked him.

"What do you mean?"

Johanna would have hit him if only she could see where he was. This ridiculous Church decree that there was no magic would have to change. It was stupid beyond belief.

He continued, "Look, why don't you go straight for home with the young boys. They'll help you over the wall and will take you to safety."

"What about you?"

"We'll go . . . the other way and keep them busy. Whatever 'they' are."

"No. There is a magical thing in the palace somewhere. We need to stay together to have any hope of defeating it."

"Go, Mistress Johanna. Please."

"Do you know what it is?"

"Go!"

At that moment a loud crack echoed through the room. The paving in the garden room split open and shafts of light blazed from under the ground. Tiles and bits of stone flew everywhere. One or two of the men used some words that they would normally never dream of using in front of a woman.

Master Willems screamed, "Go, go!"

Johanna got caught up between the men in their scramble to the wall of the room, ironically to the very place where Johanna had stood while the nobles in the ballroom were being slaughtered.

Only Master Willems remained in his position, now backlit by the eerie glow that spilled from the hole in the ground. "Go home, Mistress Johanna! Go home now!"

Standing there, in between the shivering men with chattering teeth and with her back pressed against the wall, Johanna realised several things. It was Celine's grave that had burst open, and judging by his behaviour, Master Willems knew a lot more about magic and this phenomenon than he was prepared to talk about.

Something rose out of the hole in the ground: a human shape made of glowing mist.

"It's the ghost!" a man's voice squeaked behind her.

Master Willems stood with his arms spread, chanting in a booming voice. "Begone with you, spawn of the Lord of Fire. Begone, begone, return to the depths of evil. Let the Holy Spirit smite you."

Pale and ethereal, the ghost radiated soft light. Her hair flowed over her shoulders like a waterfall. The ruffles on her dress oozed glowing mist. The pale skin on her arms glowed almost too brightly to look at. She turned her head so that Johanna could see her face.

"It's Princess Celine," a man gasped behind Johanna.

Indeed, the woman looked like she had walked off the painting of the princess that used to hang in the church, complete with the yellow dress.

Master Willems continued chanting. "The holy Triune will banish you from all the known lands . . ."

One of the young men said, "They said she haunted the palace. Why didn't I believe them?"

"Because we don't believe in ghosts?" squeaked another.

"That looks pretty real to me."

The ghosts Johanna had seen on her travels through the forest did not interact with living people. The merely repeated scenes from their lives like echoes of memories, and would never deviate from those actions. The only apparitions that interacted with the living were the partially-resurrected beings that were the result of Kylian's botched attempts at necromancy.

Her suspicions had been right: King Nicholaos had paid Kylian to perform a necromancy on his daughter because he judged his son inadequate for the throne. Kylian, despite his boasting otherwise, could not perform a full necromancy and, having seen Kylian's half-hearted results, the king might have demanded that money or favours paid for bringing Celine back to life be returned. So Kylian and his father had sent a magician to keep this annoying little king silent.

Master Willems had appeared to have temporarily run out of words. He stood, panting, facing the apparition.

"Master Willems, be careful. That's no ordinary ghost."

"Is there such thing as an ordinary ghost?" a frightened voice said behind her.

The apparition turned to Johanna.

She spoke in a voice colder than the night. "You are a usurper. You cannot leave this place with the objects that are the symbol of my father's reign."

Master Willems yelled, "Begone, spawn of evil! You are

not our beloved princess. You have no right to speak to our lady Consort like this."

The apparition took no notice of Master Willems' chanting, but continued to look at Johanna. "You're not fleeing, worm?"

"I'm not defeated that easily. The Carmine House will survive through King Roald and his heir."

"You lie!" An icy wind whirled through the room, lifting up dust and blowing it into Johanna's face.

"Begone—" Master Willems staggered back, yelling. "No, no, no!" He clamped both his hands over his face. The storm lamp crashed on the floor. Precious oil ran out of the reservoir.

"No, no, no, no!"

The cold breeze whirled up dust around him, tormenting him with images. The ghost spun threads around him, encasing him in a glowing cocoon. She was going to draw him into the grave.

Johanna groped along the ground at her feet and the wall at her back for something to use as a weapon. She found nothing except shards of pottery.

Wait—the King's staff. She dug in the sheet that she had knotted around her waist. The handle of the staff was made of wood. She pulled it out of the folds of fabric and held it before her. The wooden handle showed Johanna images of the great hall full of people cheering for the king. People who supported the royal family, nobles and commoners alike. People who were the *hope* of the kingdom.

She sprang forward, brandishing the staff. "Leave him alone. He's done nothing to hurt you."

The apparition let out a low hiss. "He's but a gibbering priest, denying his gifts."

"He's a good man and he's got nothing to do with this fight."

The ghost laughed, a horrible, wheezy sound that made Johanna's hair stand on end.

"He's got *everything* to do with the fight. It's his stupid church that my father ruined himself for that is the very cause of this fight."

Did the apparition fear the wood? Johanna took a step closer to the grave, holding out the staff's glittering gold tip.

The apparition gave another hiss, but didn't come closer.

She reached Master Willems who sat crouched on the ground, surrounded by the ghostly glow. The cocoon shook with his shivering. Johanna poked the glowing substance with the golden end of the staff. A spark zapped across the room. Then she remembered how Loesie had made a similar apparition disappear with nothing more than a willow sapling. She turned the staff around and poked the material with the wood. The cocoon parted briefly but closed back up.

The ghostly Celine reached out gnarled hands to the staff. "Give that. It's mine. It's mine."

The voice rasped and hissed, even less human than before.

Johanna plunged the handle of staff into the glowing cocoon. Glowing mist leaked from the ghost and wrapped around her hands. It was cold as the coldest of winter frost. It bit into her hands and made them numb. She yanked the staff free, shattering the cocoon into little pieces.

The ghost reached out. "Give it, give it. It's mine."

"Come and get it." She pushed Master Willems with her foot, whispering, "Come on, get up."

If only she could the apparition to touch the staff.

Master Willems groaned.

"Get up, quickly." If her previous experience was anything to go by, the apparition would change into a giant spider very soon. That also explained the abundance of spider webs in this room.

"You'll regret taunting me." Already, her voice grew raspier.

"We'll see. Come and get it."

"What are you doing?" One of the men squealed. "It will come for us now."

Johanna walked backwards, carefully so as not to trip over debris on the floor.

The ghost floated out of the grave, ignoring Master Willems who still sat on his knees, whimpering, past the shards of one of the Queen's large vases.

Behind her, the men scrambled out of the door and ran into the ballroom.

But then a different, harsh male voice echoed through that room. It sounded like Alexandre's guards had come in. There were sounds of a scuffle behind her and then a man said something in a foreign language. Burovian, Johanna thought.

The ghost hissed. It spewed a glowing thread of silk across the room.

The man yelled. Johanna couldn't see if he had been hit.

More people ran in. There was yelling and shouting. The ghost produced a sibilant hiss that made the hair on Johanna's neck stand up. The shape of Celine disintegrated into strands of mist that glowed and separated and re-formed. They grew into long limbs with long bristles. The arms and legs melted into a round body. The spider spewed glowing silk at the men like a fisherman casts a net.

Johanna lifted the staff holding it by the golden head, and waved it through the room. Threads of silk collected on the wood. They melted into dripping strands of light.

A couple of men had been caught in the strands and lay caught in cocoons on the ground. Johanna had no idea if these men were hers or Alexandre's. She waved the staff in great arcs. Magic light flew in globs around the room. It leaked down her hands and the front of her dress.

More men came into the room, and the spider was so occupied with these new people that Johanna got close. She lifted the staff and drove the wooden handle through the spider's head. It met little resistance, but the glowing mist attached to the wood. For a moment, the spider froze. Then she yanked the staff free.

The spider shattered into hundreds of little glowing pieces. They flew through the air and bounced off the ceiling and tumbled on the ground, where they slowly dimmed.

The room returned to darkness. Johanna stood there still holding the staff, panting.

Then there came the sound of footsteps of hard boots on the stone floor. A small flame appeared in the shape of a fish with a long flowing tail and delicate scales, swimming in the air. Johanna knew only one person who could do this.

Alexandre.

He had seen all the magic that she had just performed.

CHAPTER 17

JOHANNA STUMBLED away from the grave and pressed herself against the wall. It was so dark in the room that she could only see that little fish made of flames that gambolled through the air. It was a thing of mesmerising beauty, if dangerous.

She became aware of a glow of light from below: the front of her dress glowed with magic. She drew her cape over the spot to conceal it, but there were glowing spots on her hands, too, and goodness knew where else.

She had no idea where the others were. Some men had escaped into the ballroom, she hoped. Master Willems might have been smart enough to crawl to the side of the room. She clutched the wooden handle of the king's staff, doing her best to keep her breathing as quiet as possible.

The sound of footsteps from Alexandre's high-heeled boots echoed in the empty room. Johanna couldn't see him, but she felt his presence like a burning beacon. Why had the baroness ever said that Alexandre was a weak magician? Why had she ever thought that she could defeat him with a band of followers whose only weapons were their prayer books? Why did no magician want to help her? Master Willems, Loesie, Magda, all of them had refused.

She waited.

The little fire fish frolicked through the air, lighting up different parts of the room. The orange glow lit the rubble-strewn ground, where dust and broken glass revealed no signs of magic. Then it came to the middle of the room where the slab of stone that covered Celine's grave had split open. Jagged shards of stone pointed up at the ceiling. Sprays of dry earth had been cast over the floor. The grave itself was a jagged hole.

Alexandre stopped at the edge of the grave. The little fish-light frolicked around him. He wore well-polished high-heeled boots with shiny buckles, velvet trousers and a knee-length coat. A sand-coloured ponytail hung over his back.

"Hmmm," he said, and then he said something in a foreign language. His voice was cultured and sounded sharp and arrogant.

A gruff voice responded at the door to the ballroom.

Johanna looked for ways to escape. She had to get out of here before they discovered her. She was probably leaking magic and no matter how well she hid, they would discover her before they discovered the others.

But getting out required first getting past the grave. The room was narrow, with glass doors all along the left-hand side. Johanna stood against the right-hand wall, which had doors into the ballroom. She could try to sneak along the wall to the very end, where the short wall of the room consisted of glass doors. Or she could try to sneak back through the ballroom, but she had no light and, short of the palace foyer—where the doors were locked—and the forecourt—where the gates were locked as well—she knew no way of getting out of the palace.

So she took a step forward, feeling her way along the wall. Another step, and she felt the warm presence of one of the boys. She poked him and he also moved along the wall.

With every step Johanna took, she watched Alexandre. There was some sort of commotion at the far end of the room. Men spoke in foreign voices. Someone came in carrying a bright torch. By its light, Johanna could make out the silhouettes of three men in hairy cloaks. Also clearly visible were a group of people in dark clothing against the wall. Those were some of the men in her group.

Immediately, Alexandre's guards sprang into action with a lot of yelling and shouting.

Johanna pushed the man in front of her. *Hurry up, hurry up.* They made their way along the wall as fast as they dared, while one of the young men at the back screamed obscenities at Alexandre.

Johanna cringed, but a good effect of his action was that Alexandre and his fish left the area near the grave and went back to the door.

"Run," Johanna whispered to the man in front of her. She would not let the young man who was brave enough to call Alexandre names draw the tyrant's anger in vain.

They ran. Well, it wasn't a proper run, but more a fast shuffle along the wall, avoiding the pillars that supported the roof and unspecified debris that had lain there since the night that the city burned. Johanna didn't want to think about what all the things were that she kicked, trod on and crunched under her feet.

The shouting behind her intensified.

They reached the far end of the room where the glass wall came around to meet the inner wall. The first door was miraculously still intact. It also wouldn't open.

"Smash the glass," Johanna said.

"They'll hear us."

Johanna looked over her shoulder, where a couple of men with torches were coming in their direction. "That doesn't matter. Quick."

The young man kicked. Glass shattered. His mate helped him kick the glass shards out of the frame.

"Come, mistress, you first." He helped Johanna through the hole and then climbed through himself. His mate followed. His clothes caught and fabric ripped. The glow from the torches was getting stronger. By its light, she recognised the faces of the two young men with her. They were Bart and Simon, sons of the merchant Jan Hendricksen, who had not survived the fires.

"This way," Johanna said, starting down the stairs into the garden. She had inserted the staff back into the sheet around her waist.

"We're not waiting for the others?" Simon said.

"We need to get the mistress out," his brother said.

"I don't like leaving them. I didn't even see where they went."

"Outside, I hope. Come on, the Shepherd said that the most important thing is that the mistress is safe."

Johanna followed the brothers down the stairs into the darkness of the garden, past the graves of the King and Queen.

She understood why Master Willems would have instructed them in this way, but didn't like to be considered worth more than the other people. *She* didn't like the idea of running away, especially when Master Willems was still inside.

They ran in single file across the dirt-covered pavement. Sounds of a struggle drifted on the wind.

Johanna looked over her shoulder, but it was far too dark to make out anything except the glow of three lanterns bobbing as the men carrying them ran through the garden.

Johanna and the brothers reached the circular area with the benches around the empty fountain with the empty pedestal in the middle. They ran along the basin's edge, through the bushes to the garden wall. Bart climbed into the hedge and to the top of the wall. He cursed.

"What?" Simon said.

"Ladder is gone."

Simon cursed as well and then apologised. "Sorry, lady."

"I'll jump," Bart said. "It's not far."

He disappeared. Simon clambered onto the wall using the bushed, and then he helped Johanna up. It was very dark and she couldn't see where she was putting her hands and feet. Branches scratched her. The stone of the wall was cold and slippery and her fingers were fast losing sensation.

But finally Johanna sat atop the wall, balancing with one leg on either side. It was awfully dark down there on the other side of the wall.

"Jump, mistress," Bart said.

Simon jumped off and vanished into the darkness. "Come on, mistress, we'll catch you."

The lights in the garden had come much closer. Men yelled out in foreign voices and spread out to search for the escapees. Alexandre himself was coming into the garden with a creature of fire leaping next to him, a long-bodied creature, like a stoat or an otter.

Johanna jumped into the dark void.

Hands tried to catch her, but the young men couldn't support her weight and she fell hard and awkwardly on her side. The tide had come up and the beach was covered in briny water which seeped into her dress.

"Are you all right, mistress?"

Johanna scrambled to her feet. Icy cold fabric stuck to her legs. "I think so."

She took a step. Ow, her ankle. She fell against Simon.

"You're sure?" Simon asked, holding her arm.

"Just don't go too fast."

As fast as they could, they walked across the muddy beach along the water. By the light from the lighthouse Johanna saw the ladder bobbing on the waves. There was now a lot of noise on the other side of the palace wall. A man shouted in a foreign language.

Johanna and the brothers reached the pier and clambered onto the quay.

They ran to the boatshed in East Harbour where they'd started and where a number of people were waiting.

Their return was greeted with exclamations of, "Thank the Triune you are back, mistress."

Johanna made her way to the back wall where the table that Master Willems used as altar still stood. She was shivering so much that she felt like her knees would give out any moment.

Her fingers were so cold that she couldn't undo the knotted sheet around her waist.

"Let me help." Greetje came to her.

Tears pricked behind Johanna's eyes. Would she need

to tell Greetje that her husband was left behind in the palace?

The sheet came loose. Johanna put it on the table and unwrapped her parcel. People gasped when she revealed the crown and the staff.

"Hail the king!" a man shouted.

A path opened up between the people. Roald crossed the room. He was looking not at the items on the table but at her.

"Why are you wet?"

"I went to retrieve the crown and staff of the Carmine House so that you can be a proper king."

He still didn't take his eyes off her. "Why is your dress glowing?"

She looked down and, yes, her dress was still glowing.

"I'll explain later." What was there to explain except that his sister had turned into a malevolent ghost, and that his father had never trusted him? She picked up the crown. "This is yours."

Now he finally looked at it, reached out and ran his finger along the top of the crown.

She lifted it and set it, gently, on top of his head.

A number of people shouted, "Hail the king!"

Roald gave her a confused look. He reached up as if to check that the crown was indeed on his head, which it was. "Does that mean that this land is mine?"

"It does."

He took the crown off his head and handed it to her. "I don't want to be king. I don't know how. My father said I was stupid so I couldn't be king."

"And you believed him?"

He stared at her. "He's the king. He knows everything."

"Roald, you are the least stupid person in this entire kingdom."

He blinked. "How can my father be wro—"

"Your father was the dumb one." Squandering the family fortune on the church, fighting with the nobles who were responsible for the businesses in Saardam, going crazy after the death of his daughter, engaging a *necromancer*. All because he was unwilling to accept his son.

"Please put it back on. Your father is dead and he can't tell you what to do anymore. You are the king and I will help you."

He put the crown back, not entirely straight, and looked at her with his slightly confused expression. His eyes were clear and blue. He had trimmed his beard and his hair was brushed and clean.

Once she would have thought that outliving him was something to hope for. Now, she realised that she utterly loved him and the thought of losing him brought tears to her eyes.

She closed him in her arms where he stood, frozen, not sure what to do.

He protested. "My mother says—"

She put her finger to his lips. "Your mother is dead, too." And Johanna didn't like the callousness she had seen in Queen Cygna's actions. "It's about us now." And about the little baby growing inside her.

She held him close. As a rare sign of affection, he also put his arms around her.

People cheered. "Long live the King and Queen!"

It would have been a cheerful occasion if it weren't for the fact that Master Willems and the other men had not yet come back.

CHAPTER 18

THEY WAITED for a while, but Johanna was shivering so much in her wet dress that several people told her to go home.

"Go home. We don't want you to get sick, mistress."

"But they went out because of me."

"Which will have been useless if you die of cold. Please go home. We will wait." Greetje was trying to stay positive, but her face was pale and her eyes red. Bart and Simon had told her what they had seen and she knew what Alexandre could do.

Johanna hugged her. "I'm so sorry. I want to wait with you, but I'm so cold."

"Just go," Greetje said.

Johanna felt awful. This was all her fault. It had been her idea to get the crown and staff. Were a few trinkets worth this much?

She could only assure Greetje that Master Willems had not been carrying any religious items that would mark him a Shepherd.

"Oh, but he knows," Greetje said. "I've no doubt of that."

Her attitude made it all worse. It was likely that her husband was dead and she knew it.

Johanna went home with Roald and two other young men, carrying the crown and staff in the sheet. It was very late now, and the houses were dark and the streets deserted.

There was a light on in Father's study. That was odd, because Father normally went to bed early and would not let the light burn if he wasn't in the room. He hated being wasteful. They quickly walked to the back of the house, where the light in the kitchen was also still on.

Nellie and Koby sat at the kitchen table. When Johanna came in, both jumped from their seats.

Nellie cried, "Oh, mistress, there you are. I'm so glad that you're back. I thought—"

"What has happened?" Nellie's eyes were red from crying.

Tears welled in Nellie's eyes. "Your father."

Johanna's heart jumped. "What happened? Is he sick?" She could see him broken and battered after falling down the stairs or in bed and too ill to get up after taking some kind of sickness.

Nellie shook her head. "It's much worse than that. They came to the door and spoke with him and they took him away."

"Who?"

"I don't know! I didn't see it. I heard them, and I should have gone upstairs and stopped them."

"It's all right," Koby said. "They were strong men. I saw them and there was nothing you could have done anyway."

"Who were they?"

"Thugs. I didn't know the men in question, but they probably worked for the LaFontaine family."

Johanna's heart was thudding. "Where did they take him?"

"I don't know!" Nellie sobbed. "I don't know. I'm sorry, mistress. I don't know."

"It's not your fault, Nellie." Johanna hugged Nellie, tears in her eyes. She was so tired and so cold, and everything was falling in pieces around her. How long would it be before Alexandre found her? And then a thought: he probably knew she was back and would use Father to lure her out. By refusing to hand over the business, he had cut off the last way in which he could have been useful to them.

Roald came in from the door into the hallway. He said in a grave and serious voice, "We will free him. No one makes my women cry."

Johanna put an arm around him and he gave her a stern look. Angry almost. It was disconcerting, coming from him. He'd never shown any of this type of concern for other people before. "I will go up to this man and I will tell this man that I am the rightful king and that he should leave."

Koby said, "But Your Majesty, I wouldn't—"

"Thank you, Roald," Johanna said.

If only it were so simple.

But something about the sincerity with which he had said it disturbed her. They had the crown and staff. They had the Carmine cloak, even if it was more brown than carmine.

They went upstairs where Johanna put on warm night-clothes and Nellie took her wet dress. "Look at the state of it. It's got burn holes and it has ripped, too. I don't know if I can fix it, Mistress Johanna."

"Don't worry about it, Nellie."

She had enough dresses to wear.

As she lay in bed, shivering under many layers of blankets, Johanna cried for Father and Master Willems and the other men. Likely, Alexandre had known who she was the moment they had come into town.

Morning dawned bright and sunny. The temperature had dipped below freezing overnight, and rime edged the dead leaves and bare branches of the trees in the garden.

She got out of bed before Roald did and went downstairs to the kitchen where it was warm.

Greetje sat at the kitchen table, crying into her hands.

Johanna sat opposite her, accepting tea and sweet porridge from Koby and eating silently. She felt terrible. She wanted to say that everything would be all right, that getting Master Willems and Father free, if they were still alive, was as easy as sending a letter of complaint to Alexandre.

"What is . . . likely to happen now?" she asked Koby.

Koby gave her an uneasy look. "We can only guess. There was a time that the tyrant caught a group of people having a Church service. He locked them up in the dungeons under the mayor's house, and the next day, the town crier proclaimed at the markets that the prisoners would be burnt at a public execution. We went and watched, because we didn't believe that he would do it, but he did. A lot of fighting broke out, but the tyrant was prepared for this and a lot of our remaining good young men were killed. We don't know that this is going to happen again, but . . ."

Johanna felt sick. "We have to stop it."

"That's right. It's barbaric," sounded a clear voice from the door. Roald stood there fully dressed in his outdoor clothes. "They are *my* men and I will tell that man that he cannot keep doing this to my men. I'm going to tell him that right now." He turned around.

"Roald."

He turned back to the kitchen and frowned at her.

"Have some breakfast first."

He didn't move.

"You can't do anything if you're hungry." And when he still didn't move, she pulled him into the kitchen. "Sit down." She pushed him into a chair.

Koby put a bowl of porridge in front of him. "Eat that, Your Majesty. It has lots of honey."

He nodded. "I want to help."

"Eat," Johanna said. She pushed the spoon into his hand. He was really terribly determined, and that was another thing about Roald. When he had something in his mind, he was not so easily deterred.

He started eating.

"So what are we going to do?" Greetje asked.

Johanna wished she knew. She wished she had a magician willing to help her, although there probably wasn't one who could defeat Alexandre. "I guess we'll go to the markets to hear the proclamation."

Greetje nodded, tears leaking out of her eyes.

Johanna put an arm around her shoulders. "Whatever happens, we'll look after you and the little one."

"Thank you." Greetje took a shuddering breath and wiped tears from her cheeks. "Thank you," she said again.

"We'll be strong. Because nothing will ever be worth the sacrifice if we don't stand up and we don't win."

Johanna managed to convince Roald to stay at home. They were, she told him, just going to have a look to see what needed to be done. Koby said that she would light the fire in the library, but Roald showed no interest in the library today. Once he had something in his head, it was hard to get him to do something else, especially something that required him to think.

"You can help Koby with the bread," Johanna said.

And that distracted him enough to stop demanding to come. They simply couldn't risk that anyone recognised him. Men didn't usually go shopping with the women.

Johanna, Nellie and Greetje dressed in their winter clothes. Jackets, thick cloaks, hats, scarves and mittens.

They walked through the streets, pulling up their scarves against the biting wind.

There were a lot of guards at the markets. The usual line of people stood outside Alexandre's house, but there were more guards than usual, including a number of the ones who everyone called the elite guards, with bears. They were Estlander men and they reminded Johanna of Sylvan. The fact that most of them walked with bears meant that they had some magic capability themselves.

Johanna had wanted to speak to Leo Mustermans. She needed his help but didn't want to ask for it, because it would be dangerous. But there were so many guards that she didn't dare talk to him. He smiled at her when she walked past.

Johanna was between the stalls when people in the square started cheering. There was also the sound of a ringing bell. She quickly ran to a place where she could see the mayor's house.

A man had come to the top of the stairs. It was the town crier, Master Polman, who had fulfilled that role for many years. He was a thin little man with a large moustache which he twirled, as he usually did when waiting for attention.

"Listen up," the town crier said. His voice was unusually loud for a man of his size. Johanna had always thought him an arrogant little man, and that fitted his position, but the fact that he continued to work for the occupiers confirmed that his arrogance was more than a professional requirement. What had Alexandre promised him in return for his support? How easily could these ambitious men be bought? How little respect had they left after they had switched sides?

He unrolled a sheet of paper and held it up in front of him.

More and more people came from between the stalls to listen.

"Listen up, listen up!" He squinted at the paper as if unsure of what was written. "You will have heard that overnight, a group of rabble-rousers broke into the palace. They disturbed the ghosts of the people who died there. Those ghosts are now moving into the city to disturb our good citizens."

What a liar. But many people in the crowd gasped.

"Men of the guard risked their lives defending the city's property. One of the thieves was an evil magician. But do not fear. The unrest seekers have been detained. Tomorrow at noon, there will be a public punishing."

He rang the bell again and turned back into the house.

No. No, Father, Master Willems, no, no. Johanna's vision blurred. But her tears were not of sorrow. They were tears of anger. Her cheeks were burning with it. She accepted that she might get into trouble. Master Willems, too, but *Father?*

All around her, a great tumult broke out. People shouted their anger and the sound of so many voices made Johanna want to clamp her hands over her ears. But she didn't. She said to the man next to her, "If anyone wants to leave town, I have a horse for sale."

There were guards everywhere.

He frowned and then his eyes widened. "Where might this horse be?"

"It's in the warehouse next to the sea cow barn." She chose it because it was big, empty and dry. The man went around his mates and colleagues to tell them about the horse.

Johanna caught a lot of sideways glances in her direction. One or two people muttered, "Where did she get a horse?"

She just hoped that none of the guards noticed.

Johanna, Nellie and Greetje left the marketplace. Greetje was quiet, her face drawn. Nellie looked puzzled. "But mistress Johanna, I don't understand. Leo Mustermans said he'd take the horse into East Harbour."

"Shhh. It's not about the horse. It's a secret meeting."

Nellie's mouth formed a soundless "Oh". Poor Nellie. She was always so serious and never understood hidden meanings.

The three of them arrived at the warehouse not much later. A couple of people were already waiting, amongst them Master Deim and Johan and Martine Delacoeur.

Master Deim hugged Johanna. "These are grim tidings. How are you keeping up? I understand that your father is in that group as well?"

Johanna nodded. Tears were perilously close to the

surface. Father would have spent the night in a cold cell. He was old and quite frail. Maybe they hit or kicked him. And for what? Not wanting to marry Lisbeth LaFontaine?

Martine Delacoeur hugged her as well. Johanna had not expected her to be here or even to support her.

"We want Roald on the throne and we want you as a consort Queen," Martine said. "There are more of us who feel this way. King Nicholaos did some strange things that a lot of us didn't like and couldn't work with, but you are different. Roald is different. Does he even go to that church?"

That was an interesting question. Nominally, Roald went to church, but if he considered any book holy, the scriptures of the Triune were definitely not it. For now, they were united against magic and the occupation, but there was a fight against the Church of the Triune getting too much influence still to be fought.

"How are you and your husband keeping up?" Johanna asked Martine.

"Compared with you, I shouldn't complain, but Johan and my sister's husband don't get on very well. Still, we have our own room, even if it's a small one, and it's dry."

"If cold," Johan muttered, his hands in his pockets. "At times, I wonder if it's colder inside than out, in more than one way."

Martine sighed. "Yes, it's not doing the relationship between me and my sister any good."

While other people came into the warehouse asking about "the horse", Johanna slipped into the nearby sea cow barn, where it was dark and damp, but smelled of cooking. Loesie sat huddled by a small fire. She had caught a fish which she was roasting over the flames.

"I'm not coming," she said before Johanna could ask anything.

Johanna crouched. "How did you know it was me?"

"The sound of your footsteps. The feel of your magic. It has grown stronger."

That statement made Johanna uneasy. She had felt it, too. Stronger magic meant that Alexandre could feel her, too. Stronger magic meant that he might want to confront her, and there was no way she could win such a fight.

She sought excuses. "That's because I banished the ghost like you did on the bank of the river, with a willow stick. It exploded all over me." But she knew the real reason: because the child she carried was not Roald's.

"I see that magic, but I also see other changes that are deeper. You should stay away from me. You don't want my bad magic to be entangled with yours."

"Loesie, I'm imploring you to help us." If only she knew. "There will be a public execution tomorrow. Master Willems is one of the people. My father is another."

"Cowpats. Your father is an old man. What do they want with him?"

"The company. The richest inland trader in Saardam."

She snorted. "I'll never understand people with money."

"I'm not asking you to understand anything. Just help us, Loesie. Please." Tears were very close to the surface. This was all so horrible.

Loesie said nothing.

Johanna couldn't repress a wave of anger. "I thought you were my friend."

"I can't join you because you're my friend," Loesie said. "I thought I explained why."

"You did, and I understand, but we're desperate, simple as that. We *need* you." Her voice caught.

Loesie continued to stare into the fire.

The murmur of many voices reached into the barn from the hall next door. Johanna really should be going.

"Please, Loesie. I'm not asking much and I've done my best to help you despite danger to my life. If you want to repay me, come to the market place tomorrow noon."

Loesie continued her silence, so Johanna rose, but when she was at the door to the barn, Loesie said, "Wood is stronger than fire."

"No it's not. Haven't you seen the results of the fires?"

Loesie gave her an intense look. Her eyes had misted over again. "Without wood, there cannot be a fire. Remember that."

Johanna walked the short distance to the warehouse without seeing much. She didn't know what to do. There were no other magicians she could ask, nothing else she could think of doing to counter Alexandre's fire magic. Father would be burned. Master Willems would be burned.

In the large warehouse a lot more people had turned up while Johanna had been away. Not only were Church people there, but also a group of market stallholders under the leadership of Leo Mustermans. Those groups were standing in their own parts of the hall eying each other. When she came in, they formed a path to let her through. Greetje came with her, as well as Master Deim.

After the latter had called for silence, Johanna said, "I wish I had answers, but I don't. I wish I had a power magician who had a chance of defeating Alexandre, but I don't. I only have myself and the rightful king, and the hope that we will be able to emerge from this dark time. But we will not be able to stop the deaths of our loved ones without your help, and even then it may not be possible." Her voice caught. "I'm so sorry. I wish I had better news for you, but I don't." They couldn't have stayed in Florisheim, but coming back here had been a bad decision.

"I, for one, am not going stay silent if he goes ahead with the executions," a man said.

"No, me neither." This was Leo Mustermans.

Johanna said, "Then you'll all be burned. He'll burn your houses and your families."

"For you and the king, lady, it will be worth dying, because frankly we don't have much of a life now."

Johanna had no idea who this man was, but several others agreed with him.

"We'll be there tomorrow. We'll pack the market square. We'll bring anything that can be used as a weapon. We'll fight."

A lot of men went *yeah, yeah*, and clapped each other on the shoulders.

It was terrible. It was lunacy. Johanna met Martine Delacoeur's eyes with a look of despair. Martine would understand the futility of their promises, but even she looked worn out and ready to fight one last desperate battle.

Johanna went home, feeling tired and sick. Tomorrow was going to be a bloodbath.

CHAPTER 19

JOHANNA WENT HOME feeling drained and dejected. Master Deim and Greetje came with her. None of them said anything on the way back. There was no need because they all knew the situation was hopeless.

Yet it was too late to flee Saardam again. Alexandre knew of the survival of one member of the royal family and would hunt them down wherever they went. All the people who supported the royal family were here. But they could do nothing to oust the sorcerer.

It had started snowing, small powdery flakes drifting from the sky.

At home, they found a visitor in the kitchen: Julianna Nieland, seated at the table with her hands wrapped around a steaming mug of tea.

"When did you come here?" Johanna asked.

"Ko came into town and heard about the prisoners and executions. I went to plead with my brother to stop supporting this man and to ask him to reconsider, but he told me that we're all dumb for not seeing the greatness of magic; and that we can fight, but we'll all end up trampled in the mud."

"He said that, really?"

Julianna nodded. Her eyes glittered. "I don't know what's wrong with him."

"Has he forgotten how he came to his fortune, though hard work by his father? Does he care about no one?"

"He wouldn't care about a priest or your father. He's wanted the Brouwer Company for a long time."

That was true, but Johanna had thought, mistakenly, that it was a wish he'd use polite means to get.

"I hate to think that I'd wanted him to marry you so that I'd have a sister."

"You did?"

Julianna nodded.

Now Johanna felt embarrassed. She'd considered Julianna a rival, with her fancy clothes, frilly dresses and sleek combed hair. She'd thought Julianna was arrogant and thought less of her, but it had been the other way around. She hugged Julianna. There was a lot of hugging going on when there was no hope.

And then, looking over Julianna's shoulder, she met Roald's eyes. He'd been sitting by the fire in his usual spot, and she couldn't bear trying to explain the situation of hopelessness to him. They had to fight. She had no idea how, and it would probably end in her death, but she had to try.

She took a deep breath and asked Koby, "So what is likely to happen tomorrow?"

Koby described as well as she could what had happened the last time. There would be a platform built at the markets overnight, and the prisoners would be tied to posts. There would be piles of wood at their feet.

Of course this vile man used burnings as his method of execution. He was a fire wizard. He came from a place where witches were regularly burned in the past. She guessed that was why magicians had forced their way into the Belaman Church: to force the people to accept magic and to stop the witch burnings.

Johan and Martine Delacoeur came to the door, stamping snow off their shoes.

Johanna was surprised to see them, and offered them a spot at the table and tea.

Clamping his hands around the steaming mug, Johan said, "There is going to be a bloodbath no matter what. Alexandre will have gotten some stories out of those men, such as where his enemies are. They will be chasing down the Church and other dissenters. They will be chasing down those people who left but came back, like us. There is no option but to fight, and we'll do it with the weapons we have. That's why I'm here."

He drew a slate from his pocket and wrote something on it. Roald looked on with wide eyes. Johan put the slate down. At the top, he had written *Advantage*.

The pencil hovered over the slate. "Well, what do we have to our advantage?"

Greetje and Julianna gave him strange looks, but Johanna understood what he wanted: an ex-army general would objectively analyse the situation for the best action to take.

She said, "To be honest, we don't have much at all. He's got magic, he's got people with bears . . ."

Johan drew a line across the slate and wrote *Disadvantage* and underneath that, he wrote *magic* and *bears*.

That kind of summed it up, really. There was no hope. Anyone who could help had refused to do so.

The space under *Advantage* remained empty.

Johan tapped the pencil on the edge of the slate. "Failing military strength, we need numbers."

"We have the support of most people, even if many will be too frightened to openly support us, and I can't blame them."

"Then we need to give them a reason to do so."

"Any suggestions on how to do that?" She couldn't help sounding sarcastic. She had tried doing that the last few days, all to no avail. They were out of ideas, and most importantly, out of time.

He pursed his mouth. "You have the king's regalia?"

"We do."

"Do you have the Carmine cloak?"

"Yes, but it didn't like the dip in the harbour."

"Show them to us."

Johanna went upstairs where Nellie had hung up all their clothes. The cloak looked rather shabby on its own, more brown than red, but there was a pair of trousers that she had never seen Father wear in almost the same colour. And a gold dress that used to belong to her mother, a few shades lighter than the cloak.

Johanna took all of them downstairs, as well as the sheet with the crown and the staff. Koby and Nellie were surprised to see her come in with all these things, but Johan Delacoeur nodded. "I think she's got what I mean. Put them on, both of you."

Johanna took Roald, who was puzzled, to an empty servants' bedroom next to the kitchen. She slipped out of her comfortable dress and into the dress that hadn't been worn since she was a little girl. It was a dress with laces on both sides that could be let out to accommodate a woman's condition. She pulled the knots loose and helped Roald. The trousers were a bit wide, but a belt would fix that, and the velvet cloak shimmered in the light, even if it was no longer red. She gave Roald the staff, and as she touched the wooden handle, it re-played the scenes from inside the palace: the ghost, Alexandre and his fish. For some reason, Loesie's last words came to her mind. *Without wood, there is no fire.*

"Like this?" Roald said, putting the crown on his head.

She nodded, wiped some breadcrumbs out of his beard and took his arm.

There were gasps in the kitchen when they returned.

Martine cried, "Oh, he looks so much like his father!"

Nellie said, "Mistress Johanna, you really *are* with child."

Johan Delacoeur rose from his seat and bowed to her. "Your Royal Majesties, my humble self and my wife and whatever virtues we have that may be of use to you are at your service."

Going into a magical battle with nothing other than pomp and show still sounded like lunacy, but strangely, dressing up as king and queen made Johanna feel better.

Roald was still puzzled by the whole affair. He kept asking if he was now a real king, and she said that he was and had been ever since his father died.

They went upstairs and did some really silly things in the bedroom that were most satisfactory, because if one was about to be slaughtered, one was entitled to do really silly things, even if giggling would have annoyed the servants. Things got a bit rough, and they rolled off the side of the bed.

There came a knock on the door and Nellie said, "Are you all right, mistress?"

"Yes, no need to worry," Johanna said.

They were quiet after that, climbed into bed and went to sleep.

JOHANNA WOKE UP before sunrise the next morning. She slipped from the bed and got dressed while Roald still slept.

Koby was in the kitchen and greeted her wordlessly. She passed Johanna a steaming cup of tea and a bowl of porridge.

Nellie came into the back door when she was halfway eating it. "The podium is in the market square and people have begun to gather already."

Johanna nodded, wondering how Father had spent the night, and cringing at her immature behaviour with Roald last night.

"We must go upstairs and get you ready soon."

Johanna sighed. She couldn't have felt any less like getting dressed up, but pomp and ceremony were all they had. She followed Nellie up the stairs, remembering how she used to hate getting ready for festivities. That seemed kind of silly right now. If only getting ready for balls and ceremonies was her only problem.

They went into the dressing room and Johanna let

Nellie do her thing. Roald also went down for breakfast, and other people came into the kitchen, probably Martine and Johan Delacoeur.

By the time Johanna was ready to join them, she was so nervous that she was sure she would be sick.

The gold-coloured dress didn't allow for easy sitting down, so she stood in the kitchen, wondering how long it would be before the hair pins gave her a headache.

Roald got changed rather more quickly, but he came to the kitchen with all his buttons undone. Nellie gasped, but Johanna asked, "Did anyone help you put your shirt on?"

"No." His eyes were absolutely honest like a child's.

"No one helped you with your pants?"

"No."

"That's very good." It was astonishing. Roald had never managed to dress himself properly. Maybe there was hope. Maybe he could improve and manage his own life better. If they survived today.

She did up his buttons, her hands trembling. Then they waited. Time crept slowly towards midday. A couple of boys had gone to the markets and were going to come and get them, because if Johanna and Roald turned up too early, the effect would be spoiled. They could only come after the prisoners had been brought to the podium.

Johanna felt cold and sweaty at the same time. She lifted the hoops of the dress and sat down, but had to let out the sides even more because she felt constricted. And hungry and sick at the same time. Afraid that the boy wouldn't come, and then afraid that he would come.

Finally, there were fast footsteps in the back yard and the door opened. A young voice called, "They're just about to bring them out!"

The boy was Gijsbert.

Everyone rose at the same time. Johanna picked up the crown from the table and set it on Roald's head. Nellie draped the Carmine cloak over his shoulders.

Gijsbert went out first, then Nellie and Sebastian the groundsman in his Sunday finest. Then Roald with Johanna, flanked by Martine and Johan Delacoeur. Johan wore his uniform jacket and carried a sword.

Koby and Greetje brought up the rear.

So they walked out the back yard. They weren't even halfway down the street when the first people noticed Roald.

"It's the king!" someone yelled, and people came to the doors and windows.

There was cheering and clapping and the shouts preceded the group down the street.

The king is back. The king is back and *We have a Queen.*

"Come with us to the markets," Johanna said.

"There is a burning at the markets," a woman said. "I will not be so cruel to let my children watch that." And indeed most of the people who had come out of the houses were women or children and old people.

"We're going to stop it," Martine said. "Come and join us."

A few came, and then a few more, and then a great flood of people came talking, chatting behind them. Women carried brooms, men carried shovels or picks, or the occasional pitchfork, whatever use one had in town for a pitchfork.

And so the stream of people flooded into the market square.

A great number of people already stood there, mostly the men of the families. The beggars had abandoned their line to the steps of the mayor's house, the stall holders had left their stalls.

The prisoners were being led up onto the podium in front of the mayor's house. First were the young men who had been at the palace with her. Greetje gasped next to Johanna. Master Willems was wearing a grey sack. His arms and legs were blue with the cold and bore welts from where he had been hit. One of his eyes was swollen. After him came an older woman. She walked in stiff steps, as if she'd been beaten, and blood had seeped into the back of her shift. Her body was broken but she had the most vicious look in her eyes. As she turned towards the audience, Johanna recognised her: Helena the whore who lived in the harbour and served the sailors at night and told girls about *those things* during the day.

Then came Father. Where the others had stumbled up the steps, he kept his back straight, even though Johanna could see that walking hurt him a lot. They had allowed him to keep his trousers and shoes. Maybe they hid welts on his skin. He almost tripped over the top step. A guard grabbed his arm to keep him upright and dragged him across to one of several posts that stood lined up on the platform.

People at the front cheered, but there was no joy in their cheering. A number of guards stood at the ready, facing the crowd and scanning all who were there. Checking if the people cheered as instructed.

A couple of bears lay on the edges of the platform.

By now, people at the back of the crowd were starting to notice Johanna and Roald and the rest of the newcomers.

Johanna held Roald's arm in a tight grip. She could feel the muscles under his arm tense up and relax and tense up and relax . . . She was sure that he would love to run, or start swaying.

The people opened up a path through the crowd.

There was cheering and clapping.

A cold wind tore through the square, tearing at hats and scarves. A strand of hair escaped Johanna's bun and blew across the face. She shivered. There was magic in the air.

Alexandre had come up on the stage. He now looked into the crowd. Johanna knew that he knew where she was.

"Hail the king, hail the queen!"

"We're saved!"

More and more people came to look. They pushed others aside and formed a guard of honour across the square to the podium. One of the trumpeters, in Alexandre's blue colours, rushed to the procession and played the *King's Hail*.

And so the procession crossed the markets and there they stopped, because they met a wall of Estlander guards with bears.

Alexandre jumped down the platform and wrestled himself between his men.

The trumpeter again played the short burst of notes that was the King's Hail.

Johan Delacoeur shouted, "Make way for his royal highness King Roald and his consort Johanna Brouwer!"

The whole of the audience broke out in a deafening cheer.

By now, Alexandre had come to the front of the line of guards. "What's this?" He snorted. From close up he was taller than Johanna had expected, or maybe that was because of his high-heeled boots. His eyes were green, his face quite coarse-skinned and narrow, his hair curly and brown. He wore his customary blue trousers and a cape of the same colour, held at the top with a gold clip.

He eyed Johanna up and down and then turned to Roald. His gaze rested on the crown and staff. His expression closed. He knew these were the real items and Roald was the real heir to the throne. And maybe one of his men had lied to him about Roald having drowned in the harbour and maybe he was beating himself in the head about believing it.

Baron Uti had known about Roald. Apparently his friendship with Alexandre was not as good as Alexandre suggested in the letter to the Baron that Johanna had seen while they were in Florisheim.

Johanna stepped forward. "Thank you for taking care of our town while we were away."

Several people in the crowd laughed. Alexandre glared at them.

"We will now take over as lawful descendants of Saarland's royal family." She had expected to be sick with nerves when facing him, but she felt strangely calm.

Alexandre simply stared at her. Then he said something in a low voice in Burovian to a man at his side. This man, not a guard but a fellow noble, judging from his clothing, pushed between the guards and a moment later, he came back with a dark-haired man in a dark coat with a hideously frilled white shit underneath. Octavio Nieland.

He seemed to be taken aback at the sight of the crown. Maybe he had looked for it but had been chased out of the palace by Celine's ghost.

"This is certainly a . . . surprise." His voice was as haughty as ever.

"I'm undecided if it's a surprise."

He raised one eyebrow.

"Am I surprised that you joined the invader's men?"

"You don't understand at all."

"Oh?"

"This is much bigger than the petty grievances of this ridiculous church of yours."

"It's not *my* church and I'm beginning to think that forbidding magic is not a bad thing at all. How many people have been killed through it? Oh, you don't care because they were all common people."

He went red in the face. His hand wandered to his belt where he carried a sword.

Then he looked aside, his eyes widening. Julianna had come to the front. Like Johanna and Roald and others, she had dressed in the best clothes she had. Her hair was done up in a big bun, and her eyes blazed with anger.

Octavio laughed, in an uncomfortable way. He let his hand fall away from his belt. It was a subtle gesture, but it told Johanna one thing: he might not care much about Roald, but he definitely cared for his sister.

"There is no need for conflict," she said. "We are Saarlanders. We've solved our problems without fighting for a long time." One of the reasons that Johan Delacoeur was an *ex*-army general. King Nicholaos didn't put much effort into his armed forces. "But the invaders must go. We don't need any foreigners to run our country."

"What do you know of the menace that faces us?"

"The Church of the Triune has been elevated to menace? It justifies killing and burning down half the town?"

He threw his head back and laughed. "You know nothing at all."

"Then tell us. But while you do that call off this silly spectacle."

"These people are criminals."

"My father? The only crime he has committed is to be your competitor."

Alexandre said something in Burovian that sounded sharp and impatient.

"What is he saying? Why can't he speak to us directly?"

Roald said, "He says that he has no time for talking."

Alexandre came forward and shouted Burovian words in Roald's face. Roald, true to his nature, did not flinch. He replied in Burovian and Alexandre shouted more loudly at him.

People all around cried out in protest.

Roald turned to Johanna. "He says that—"

"What does it matter what he says. What matters is this!" Octavio gestured wildly in the direction of the harbour.

People gasped and exclaimed profanities and covered their mouth with their hands. What Johanna had taken as a reaction to the argument was . . . something else.

A few people moved aside so that she could see over the water out the heads to the east, where the Saar River flowed towards the ocean.

On the water which looked like silver with the reflecting sunlight came a ship like none she had ever seen.

It was tall like an ocean faring vessel, but in place of sails, it had a tall protuberance which spewed smoke like a chimney.

Everyone around her was shouting. Some invoked prayer, others reached their hands to the heavens and chanted. Most people just stared with wide eyes. How did the ship move? How, if it was made from wood, did it not catch fire? How, if it was made from metal, as some suggested, did it float?

Magic, people suggested, and the sea breeze carried a familiar prick.

Octavio said, "Those are the eastern traders. They've been around this area for a while and they're not coming for a cup of tea. I'm hoping, since you seem determined to retake the city before they can set foot on this land, that you have brought strong magicians."

CHAPTER 21

EVERYTHING THAT had happened over the last months suddenly made sense.

This *machine* was what the Guentherite order had been trying to recreate. This was what the iron was for.

And this was why they wanted control of Saardam, why they were building the strange thing in the harbour, and similar things all along the river, and why they needed to get rid of a church that didn't allow its followers to practice magic.

While she had been talking to Octavio, several things had happened. The young men whose task it was to make use of the distraction to go to the platform had arrived there. On the platform, the prisoners were too far away from Johanna and the group to hear what had been said, and they couldn't see the water because the mayor's house was in the way. They were confused about what was happening, frowning at each other and trying to see past the guards, who also appeared to have lost interest in their charges and appeared equally confused.

Over the heads of the people between her and the podium, Johanna spotted one of the boys trying to climb the podium, boosted up by a mate. A bear jumped up, growling.

All of a sudden the guards' attention was back where it should have been. They shouted and pulled weapons.

The boy dropped himself off the platform and hid by pressing himself against the side. But a few Saarlander guards came from the other side and tried to drag him away.

Alexandre uttered a cry of frustration. He turned back to the podium. His men made a path for him. He shouted something in which Johanna picked up the Burovian word for *kill*.

The prisoners' eyes widened.

Father was looking out over the crowd. He knew that Johanna was amongst all those people somewhere. He would have heard the King's Hail. The young man next to him was pulling on his arms, tied around the post at his back. He was shouting at the top of his voice—inaudible to Johanna over the tumult in the square—but his eyes bulged with fear.

Someone from behind fired an arrow while seated on another fellow's shoulder. It struck the bear between the eyes.

"Good shot!" someone shouted.

Johanna raised her fist. "Come on! Free the prisoners!"

Alexandre had almost reached the podium but turned around again. Seeing the crowd surge forward and one of his bears sprawled on the floor, his expression grew hard.

He raised his hand—

No. Johanna knew what would happen.

A snake made of fire sprung out of mid-air. It coiled

over the heads of the onlookers and set the pile of wood at the feet of the prisoners alight with a fleeting touch.

All of a sudden everyone was screaming.

People were running away from the fire creature, other people were trying to hit the flames out with their jackets. It was a futile activity and they only succeeded in setting fire to their clothes.

A sudden wind came up. It whipped through the square and tore at hair and hats. One of the market stands was blown over. Instead of fanning the flames, the wind blew them out. Alexandre waved his hand at the pyre, but the wind blew the flames out again.

What . . .

Master Willems. He was the only one with wind magic. He stood with his face turned up at the sky, praying.

Alexandre conjured a bigger snake.

Greetje was crying at the top of her voice. "Do something. Somebody, free my husband!"

Father was looking straight at Johanna over the heads of the crowd.

Some people tried to run away, others tried to reach the prisoners. The guards didn't seem to know what to do and seemed to decide to just defend themselves.

Roald was shouting at the top of his voice, but even standing near him, Johanna couldn't make out what he said. His face shone with sweat.

Johanna remembered Loesie's words. *Wood is stronger than fire. Fire needs wood to burn.*

She meant wood *magic* was stronger than fire magic.

But was it really? Wet wood didn't burn. Live wood didn't burn. She remembered pieces of wood sprouting leaves when Duke Lothar had performed the exorcism on Loesie.

Alexandre was not a strong magician, the Baroness Viktoriya said. Johanna had wood: the handle of the king's staff. A lot of other people in the market square had wood, too. They had brooms, and the broom heads were made up of twigs. They had shovels with wooden handles. They had pitchforks and garden rakes. Master Willems controlled the wind.

Johanna took the staff from Roald's surprised hands. "Hail the king!" she called out, holding the staff over her head.

A few people in the chaos around her repeated her, and then more and even more. The chant spread over the market place like an ink stain.

Hail the king, hail the king.

Roald himself was shouting as hard as everyone else, apparently not quite clear on the fact that *he* was the king.

As they chanted, people held their brooms or shovels over their heads.

Master Willems still held his face turned up to the sky. His lips moved in prayer.

The people shouted, "Hail the king!"

Johanna held the king's staff in the air, willing it to spring into life. The fire snake dived in and out of the woodpile at the post where Master Willems stood. The wind whirled around him, putting out the flames as fast as the fire snake could light them. Gusts of wind drew sparks and strands of fire away from the creature, threatening to dissolve it.

Johanna spurred the wind on. *Come on, come on.*

The wood of the staff *moved* under her hands. Buds sprouted between her fingers. While she watched, vines grew and sprouted leaves.

A man shouted. His shovel had turned into a bush. He

dropped it, but it hung in midair from fast-growing vines that extended faster than a man could walk.

All around, shovels, picks and pitchforks had also sprouted leaves. Brooms turned into living forests of glowing, snaking vines.

They reached the platform and intertwined with the wood from the woodpile. And that wood started sprouting, too. The fire snake whirled around so fast that it was hard to see where it went. Because the wood was alive, it could no longer make it burn. It only produced lots of smoke, which in turn made it harder to see.

Alexandre had climbed up on the platform and was throwing fire directly at the prisoners, but each time the wind blew the flames away.

A vine sprouted from the boards of the platform and twined around his leg. He roared with anger and cut it with his sword, but a new one grew, and another one around his other leg.

The boys were back on the platform, because the bears were busy swatting away sprouting leaves. They cut Master Willems free. He collapsed on the boards.

"Come, someone help carry him!"

Then Father. He rubbed his wrists. His face looked pale, but he was able to walk away by himself. A couple more boys assisted him down the platform. No one took any notice of Alexandre's guards, who were trying to tackle the encroaching greenery by hacking away with their swords. But Alexandre's legs were already rooted to the platform's boards, held there by thick vines. He was screaming at his men and they hacked at the wood, but it grew faster than they could cut it.

The vines crept up his torso, scrunching his jacket between wooden coils and his ribcage.

"Let me out of here, witch!"

Johanna finally lowered the staff. All the vines detached themselves and hung limp, as if the magic had just fled.

She climbed on the platform. Father watched her with wide eyes.

Alexandre's face was red splotched with white. His eyes bulged. His breathing was fast. He whispered, "You common whore."

Johanna spat in his face.

"You thought we were all killed?" she said in a low voice. "You thought you could scare the people of Saardam into supporting you? Well, you can, for a short time maybe, but if you really knew the people of this town, you'd know that they won't support tyrants."

He laughed in a breathless, wheezing fashion. "I . . . am . . . not . . . the enemy."

"You've done an excellent job so far behaving like you are."

"All . . . the . . . lowlands will fall . . . to . . . eastern magic."

"Rubbish," Father said. "They're *traders*. They come to sell things."

"We . . . can only . . . face them if we have . . . magic."

"We seem to have plenty of that ourselves."

"That . . . evil church—"

"I will hear nothing more of the church!" Johanna spat at him again. "None of your reasons justify the killing of thousands and the burning of entire cities. Not just us, but Aroden and all the villages along the river. This was never about the church. It was about power. You wanted Saardam so that *you* could negotiate with these eastern traders for this *machine* of theirs. *You* are just a power-hungry, greedy, sad excuse for a prince. You sowed fear into the hearts of all and then destroyed what people built in your name."

"I didn't . . ." His gasps came very fast now. Despite the fact that Johanna had detached the staff from the vines, the ones that held him were still tightening their grip.

"You didn't betray the very people you recruited? You didn't conjure fire dragons that destroyed the Guentherite abbot's summer residence?"

"They were . . . rebellious."

"That justified the deaths of many men?"

The vines constricted his chest so much that he couldn't speak. His face grew ever darker in colour. Spit dribbled from his mouth where his tongue had swelled so much that it stuck out between his teeth.

He lived—just—but if she couldn't stop the will of the vines to kill this man, then nothing could. She turned around because she didn't want to see this. Already, her stomach churned with revulsion.

Father was free, Master Willems had been reunited with Greetje, the other prisoners were free, and that was all that mattered. The men who had supported Alexandre had fled to the harbour and were using one of the Nieland ships to flee. She presumed Octavio was on it.

As she walked down the steps of the former platform that had become an intertwined tangle of trees, there was an awful gasp and gurgle from behind her. Turning around, she already couldn't see Alexandre anymore, but she assumed that he had become one with the trees.

The people in the square now all gathered to watch the harbour. While Alexandre's men fled, the strange eastern ship had come closer. It was a dark, square, menacing-looking thing, with smoke belching from the chimney. It was too far away to see any people on deck, but it was about to come into the harbour, and the Nieland ship was about to go out.

Both vessels halted.

A great tide of people started making their way to the harbourside, where they could see. Johanna and Roald were swept up to the front of that surge.

Had they deposed of a tyrant only to be faced with a worse opponent?

But the two ships had settled into a standoff and nothing happened. The people dispersed. Johanna asked some of her young men to keep watch and come to warn her as soon as something changed.

She and Roald walked home over the markets, where an entangled bit of bush marked Alexandre's last position. At least the growth appeared to have slowed.

At home, Father was in the kitchen, eating with trembling, sore-riddled hands. Johanna hugged him and cried on his shoulder. He was so thin. But his eyes shone with happiness.

"We're free now. You're the queen."

Never mind that she had no idea how long that would last.

Nellie came into the kitchen, and Greetje, as well as Johan and Martine Delacoeur. They had a celebration of sorts. Johan talked about fixing up the palace, but that would need removal of Celine's ghost. Johanna was too tired to even think of that.

She followed Roald to bed. There was no romping around and giggling tonight. She fell asleep as soon as her head hit the pillow.

～

It was still dark when someone knocked on the door.

"Mistress?" It was Nellie.

Johanna stuck her feet out of the warmth of the bed. Oh, it was so cold! She tiptoed to the door and opened it a crack. Nellie stood in the hallway with a candle.

"There is a young man in the kitchen for you."

Johanna quickly got dressed and felt her way down the stairs. The lights were on in the kitchen, and Koby was kneading dough. By the heavens, was this the time she normally got up?

At the table opposite Koby sat a young men whom Johanna recognised as one from the church.

"Has anything happened?"

"I'm afraid it has. You best come quickly."

Johanna followed him into the darkness, which wasn't quite as dark as she expected. The sky had a distinct blue tinge on the eastern horizon.

They walked in silence to the harbour. There was no longer a need to be afraid of guards or bears, but the dark realisation grew in Johanna's mind that this might be a temporary solution.

Even before they had come to the quay, Johanna already noticed the orange glow that lit the buildings on the quay that was not morning light.

Something was on fire in the mouth of the harbour, sending smoke billowing over the water. The orange light glinted off the metal side of the eastern ship.

A couple of men stood on the quay watching the spectacle.

"What happened?" Johanna asked.

"We can't be sure, mistress. The one man who saw it is rambling about dragons, and none of it makes any sense. We sent him home. Maybe he'll be clearer tomorrow."

Dragons. In the proper use of the word, they were creatures from the far east. Not lizards, which could also be called dragons, but large winged creatures that spewed fire.

Johanna eyed the foreign ship and its menacing shape. The burning object that had to be the remains of the Nieland vessel was slowly sinking under the surface.

"Am I mistaken or are they coming this way?"

"You're not mistaken, mistress. They're coming into port."

A Word of Thanks

THANK YOU very much for reading *Fire Wizard*. The story is not finished here! In the next book, *The Dragon Prince,* the eastern traders come to Saardam. Baron Uti isn't the only leader who wants their magic and strange machines, nor the only one prepared to go to war to get what he wants.

As author of this book, I would appreciate it very much if you could return to the place where you purchased this book and leave a review. Reviews are important to me, because they help readers decide if the book is for them.

ABOUT THE AUTHOR

Patty Jansen lives in Sydney, Australia, where she spends most of her time writing Science Fiction and Fantasy.

Her story *This Peaceful State of War* placed first in the second quarter of the Writers of the Future contest and was published in their 27th anthology. She has also sold fiction to genre magazines such as Analog Science Fiction and Fact, Redstone SF and Aurealis.

Patty has written over twenty novels in both Science Fiction and Fantasy, including the *Icefire Trilogy* and the *Ambassador* series.

pattyjansen.com

BOOKS BY PATTY JANSEN

MORE INFORMATION:

PATTYJANSEN.COM